Bliss
Mountain

by

Aashish Kaul

Finishing Line Press
Georgetown, Kentucky

Bliss
Mountain

ACKNOWLEDGMENTS

The author gratefully acknowledges the support received from the following during the completion of this book:

Department of English, University at Albany, SUNY; Dr. Nuala McGann Drescher Program, New York; and the Swedish Collegium for Advanced Study, Uppsala.

Excerpts from the following works are quoted with permission of the publishers:

MEMOIRS FROM BEYOND THE GRAVE: 1768-1800 by François-René de Chateaubriand. Translation Copyright © 2018 by Alex Andriesse. Reprinted by permission of New York Review of Books. All Rights Reserved.

"The Envoy" from GIVEN SUGAR, GIVEN SALT: POEMS by Jane Hirshfield. Copyright © 2001 by Jane Hirshfield. Reprinted by permission of HarperCollins Publishers. All Rights Reserved.

"The Magic of Mantovani" from SELECTED POEMS by Michael Hofmann. Copyright © 2008 by Michael Hofmann. Reprinted by permission of Farrar, Straus and Giroux. All Rights Reserved.

"Arrival at the Waldorf" from THE COLLECTED POEMS OF WALLACE STEVENS by Wallace Stevens. Copyright © 1942 by Wallace Stevens; renewed 1982 by Holly Stevens. Reprinted by permission of Penguin Random House. All Rights Reserved.

Publisher: Leah Huete de Maines
Editor: Christen Kincaid
Cover Art: Steve Johnson
Author Photo: Apara Tayal
Cover Design: Elizabeth Maines McCleavy

Order online: www.finishinglinepress.com
also available on amazon.com

Author inquiries and mail orders:
Finishing Line Press
PO Box 1626
Georgetown, Kentucky 40324
USA

Contents

In the memory of my father

Wir sind nichts; was wir suchen, ist alles.
—Hölderlin

The Coach and The Spire

I

I arrived in the valley at the height of summer. After three overcast days in New York, I took the train north along the Hudson. An ocher haze hung low over the cliffs at that hour. But between the villages of Sleepy Hollow and Briarcliff Manor—the gothic or idyllic echoes compounding the mood—the clouds briefly dissolved, and the sun came out. It made an impression, this sudden light filling the scene, cutting deep through strata of memory. The Hudson widened here and with a white stationary yacht in the middle gave the appearance of a cove or a lake.

Two unconnected images, images from different hemispheres really, from very dissimilar periods of my life, rose up to the surface then.

A view of the bay from beneath the broadleaved shade of the figs bordering the promenade on Sydney's Balmoral Beach. Those large trees with an oddly comforting familiarity were a reminder of my happy childhood in India. Their old-world air amidst the voguish signs branded into the landscape had calmed my stranger's nerves at the time. All day long I had stared at the glittering Pacific trying to loosen my grip on the past, to look clearly at my surroundings, make preparations to begin again. Far away on this edge of earth, among beings who appeared secure in the abstract certainties of language and culture, which time and distance had worked mysteriously to solidify rather than weaken. But what looked fixed and settled on the circumference, quivered easily in the dry inland air. Voices dwindled, lettering became sparse, and a remote sublimity entered physical forms. Antiquity flattened differences here; to stand apart was to be superfluous. And beyond the marble gum and the mulga and dunes of spinifex, the ancient heart of the savannah flared scarlet and black in the declining sun.

The other, more recent, image was from the town of Keswick in Cumbria, where over two hundred years ago the English Romantic poet Samuel Taylor Coleridge had made his home and spent some of his best days. I had come up the grassy knoll adjacent to the empty marina immediately south of the town and was granted the vision just ahead of Rita's solemn figure, the black windbreaker bunched at the waist and reaching to her thighs making her appear at once stylish and small, as she gazed at the cloud-kissed surface of Derwentwater. *Der Wanderer über dem Nebelmeer.* Wanderer above the mist. Wanderer above the sea of fog. I paused to regard Rita's silhouette turned away from me and surveying the scene. Mist spread low over the water and the green-domed islands, but further up the air was clear, showing the fells, wooded at ground level but ashen and bare and streaking fluorescent on the inclines, that ringed and fingered the lake. Lone dark clouds slowly drifting eastward were outlined a deep orange by the last ray of the sun. High above, the sky was slate-gray, except in a few places where the shroud seemed to have thinned, giving to these oblong patches a curious mauve flush.

The train was now moving at the level of the river, up close, so that the impression was of being on a boat or a trawler. Then the train curved inward and rows of trees hid the river. Later, it found the river again and, in the distance, you could see the land slicing the water in a green curve outlined by yellow sand.

My thoughts returned to my wife. The woman looking at the lush scene with such calmness, what cares lay heavy on her heart? The stillness of the scene—but perhaps solitude, with its suggestive voluptuousness, would be a better word—this immense Lake District solitude rose up to meet her. She turned and for a quick moment her face and eyes were heavy with the elements; a contrast of emotions scrambled for purchase, but left behind only a touch of confusion, a slightly startled expression. I tried to look away. We were still skittish around each other. The moist breeze felt fleshy to the touch. A mute swan floated close to the marina. The orange bill bordered by a dark patch in a melting puff of white. And then suddenly, as if tipsy with kisses like in that Hölderlin poem, it dunked its head into the water. Oh, my love, I wondered, my sweet love, what have I done to the dream of you?

Young sycamores and beeches rising from the weeds that lined the riverbank. Red and black brick buildings holding their sharp lines. The bluffs veiled in the river mists falsely suggesting the sea to the north.

Three days of mostly low skies, cloudpressed into those humid Manhattan avenues, their gray air full of varicolored striations of movement, I had been riven by conflicting emotions. Crushed and jostling like apples down a chute, Dos Passos had called his fellow New Yorkers.

Now with the famed skyline half lost in mist, the stifling image behind the metaphor was laid bare. Moving in right-angles through a subterranean maze of concrete cuboids, the lightning vision of a fuchsia dress trailing against a stone façade as the sibylline form ahead turned west on Forty-Ninth seemed to splash across some forgotten memory and left me on the verge of tears.

New York was nothing without its sky, the French writer Albert Camus had bitterly noted in an essay from the Forties. Solid words. I should have remembered them. They would have fitted my mood, tamed it. In those first days, however, the sky could be glimpsed only at night, indigo-black behind pale clouds floating low and swift across it, and the moon above the East River, large but ungenerous, withdrawn unto itself and throwing the island into somber relief. Then it was almost pleasant to watch the darkness fall from above and fill the countless ravines, and the towers in the distance dimly aglow with numerous spots of gold deep in their interiors. If by day the rains sharpened the feeling of exile and separateness, then the nights, homogenous, connected to the empyrean, released a sentiment of slow homecoming.

But the sentiment just then was perhaps misleading, fed by the long journey begun years ago, by the new sights crowding out the old, by the pressing need to rest a little.

In a different age, the city's vertical lines thickening out of the morning mist must have quickened the pulse of passengers entering the harbor. With inflamed minds—the tiredness eclipsed for now by the promise of future rewards, felt like a pinprick between breaths—they must have hurriedly climbed ashore, over rocks of mica schist and gneiss a billion years old. Formed in the tectonic drama that had shaped much of the eastern seaboard and that had left New York with one of the longest natural harbors in the world, the strategic significance of which had not been lost on the first Dutch settlers, the foundations of these modern erections, whose gothic traceries and glittering spires touched the skies with a brash exuberance and doused the crepuscular streets below with untold passions, were in fact layered in deep time.

So a dizzying geological pastness had anchored all this freedom and ambition. An old stillness prevailed here, felt at times in the long shadows cast by the buildings on the sidewalk or in the hush interior of rooms more suited to the night than to the day—a stillness that again and again entered the heart and pushed one to find comfort in the open.

The steamships were long gone, and my prosaic Atlantic crossing had been completed in a matter of hours. And because this was so, I was given a different, almost an insider's vision of the place.

Not the harbor, not the fog churning and fingering the city into being, but vast tracts of land and rock and reed-beds stretching westward, expanding into the fluid horizons of America. There the sun was strong, and a gentle massing of clouds could be seen in the north. To the east, the earth felt heavy and compressed; the undulations of its surface quickly tightening into folds of tiered rock all the way to the edge of the Hudson, broken here and there by concrete office blocks, hotels, and open parking lots. Further ahead, beyond the wall of the Palisades, the serrated skyline of Manhattan was now and then visible across the dip of the river. In the afternoon haze, its scale seemed oddly diminutive, as in a child's cardboard cut-out, and nothing romantic, freshening one's impressions, like the view afforded a traveler coming by sea.

The taxi was moving through the system of motorways built over the watershed of the Hackensack River. The strip of ground seen past the loop of the motorway revealed old scars and hinted at cycles of harm done over generations. These wetlands, once teeming with life, had soon enough endured the not uncommon fate of forming the periphery of a metropolis in making. In its lower stretches, the Hackensack, home to the perch and the herring in the old days, had until recently suffered extreme pollution, and the land still gave the forlorn look of a place where different industrial urges had been taken up and later abandoned.

The road curved to the right and, across the steady stream of traffic flowing in the opposite direction, one saw the empty rail tracks, shining like so many silver streams in a bed of rust, cover the grassy earth with a mood of sad neglect. As the sight traveled backward to the point where the tracks converged, there rose sheer into the sky the tall structures of the city, suddenly very big and imposing.

Everything gave the stripped-down look of extreme functionality which the open vistas, now firmly behind me, heightened still further. The setting, almost an archetype, filled me with foreboding. It had the aura of a long cycle ending badly. I felt I was witnessing a moment from a novel I had read in my adolescence. The memory I was searching for did not come to me until much later, and when it did, I was less alarmed than ashamed. The shame was misplaced, fleeting. But the premonition had been correct. From that day, I started to pay close attention to a world I had for years neglected, half deliberately and half out of boredom.

The driver's voice filtered through my thoughts. He said he had skipped the Holland for the Lincoln where traffic was quicker. He was late in speaking, but how was I to know? He was being courteous, and this courtesy was flattering. Perhaps he had taken me for a local, perhaps distinctions of this sort were useless here.

The tight space between the rocks of Weehawken widened and just before the bend in the road as it sloped down into the tunnel the view cleared. Directly ahead the downtown buildings formed an enormous cone, angling up from the edge of water to where the glass walls of the Freedom Tower soared steep into the sky. Diligent hands and silent lips pursuing ideal forms in a logic of hierarchies and money had, within a few years, raised this thing seventeen hundred feet into the sky. I felt a quickening of the pulse. Someone had finished the painting by Pieter Bruegel the Elder and transplanted it on earth.

On clear winter nights, the prospect was subtler, more magnificent. Outlined by the black waters of the estuary, this modern-day Babel shone in a darkness that quivered like aether around a flame. If only Fritz Lang could have seen it like this: his vision of the dystopian metropolis at once realized and surpassed! And in contrast to the silly, formulaic maneuvers of the film, its absurdly impressive structures concealing a childishly simple message, reality had turned out to be both fuller and more intricate. Solemn and impressive that shimmer of light like some distant galaxy twinkling away in soundless space. And the countless wills, clashing and cancelling out one another in the *heart machine* of the city, issuing a deep funereal calm into the sky.

Rita had extended her stay in London by a week, but she had managed to find for me at this time of the year a studio apartment in a remodelled townhome near Gramercy Park.

From the very beginning, from our first youthful days together, I had been awed by this aspect of her personality. She knew her way in the world, and the world in turn yielded unfailingly to her wishes. Because this was so, she believed it to be the case with everyone, something which in the first years of marriage was often a cause for quarrels between us. She had natural confidence and style, and though dainty looking, her presence didn't go unnoticed in any gathering. Her manners were polished, and her bearing had a touch of old nobility, of the kind one read about in novels of that period. She had a delicate nose and slim psychic hands, while her high cheekbones agreeably deflected attention away from the slight fleshiness of the face.

I never once heard Rita boast in public or private. When left alone she was prone to strangely naïve reveries, and yet, she was an extremely practical person. By extension, the fall of a dress, the incline of a shoe, the movement of an arm—each of these events submitted to that impressive blend of order and refinement. Slowly, in my imagination, she had grown to embrace the older meaning of her name: in Sanskrit, it suggested the order that ruled the universe.

For all that, her cool demeanor became at times too vexing to ignore. Then, hardly able to keep my own artistic pieties in check, I would end up by saying something hurtful. She had both kindness and virtue but was unwilling to extend her imagination to abstract ideals. I could never tell how seriously she took my advice, although she rarely acted without first hearing it.

The West Side lay heavy with tourists at that hour and moving cross-town into the lengthening shadows had brought on a cooling relief.

I liked the place Rita had selected for me. The lobby had period and rococo flourishes, and my room, with a dash of modern flair, included a kitchenette and French windows that led to a narrow balcony. In the free space between buildings was a little garden with two appropriately sized flowering trees to tempt the finches, and the stone patio along one wall echoed with their song throughout the day. Inside, the dark, gilt-edged lampshades obtained a charm beyond their means, while the bathroom, with an incompatible Nordic vibe, looked hurriedly finished.

I thought of calling Rita. She was at a party in Marylebone. One of her friends from the days she had lived in London had just been made partner at her old firm. She said: 'I have lost my taste.' At first, I took it literally. Then, distractedly, she let more words fall from her lips: 'My heart is lost, Gir; the beasts have swallowed it.'

Dramatic emotions from another age, out of pitch in the contemporary ear, the scale falsifying the feelings.

Rita was not given to poetic excesses, so to hear my name in a string of nineteenth century romantic verse was mildly unsettling. To tell her this would have been pointless. I knew she had spoken reflexively and not to catch my attention. Speaking merely for effect was not in her nature. But from where then had she picked up this kitschy bit of Baudelaire?

Among the books by my bedside in Sydney was an old anthology of French poetry. On a warm summer night, while I was away in India tending to my sick father living out his final winter, did she at long last cross that insurmountable gulf and reach for the volume? I had a vision of her easing her ennui by lamplight. Outside the large awning window, possums are frolicking in the red gum. The first cool southerlies arrive, scudding luminous clouds past southern constellations stretched firm on their star-pegs. The pale velvety petals fall into her moist heart with a weak shudder.

The evening was starting to pool beneath the trees, but the sky, raked by the sun's rays, was ribbed with light. I became aware of birdsong steadily cleaving through my thoughts. I took a shower and went out into the street.

At the end of Irving Place was the private park, smaller than a block, that gave its name to the neighborhood. Here was a piece of classic London in the bosom of the New World. The airy calm of the spot, heightened further by the empty fenced-in garden whose exclusivity worked like a charming paradox, brought to surface memories and disappointments that were still fresh in me.

A little over twenty-four hours ago, on the last day of my stay in England, I had thought of tracing a route I had walked often in the summers of my youth. From Soho to Bloomsbury, then crossing Tottenham Court Road and, moving awhile between smooth Georgian façades with arched doorways and stuccoed lower floors, coming to rest in Regent's Park. My step was swift, the buoyancy of my illusions and my youthful ardor hardly ever allowed a moment's pause. I was seldom tired in those days, for I kept one eye turned inward, ready to catch the spark I might have kindled to flames under that lucid English sky.

Each time I ended up further afield. From the corner of Primrose Hill, for instance, taking the towpath lined with narrowboats to the footbridge at Camden Lock, where, between the willows, people often settled to catch the sun. Then skirting the market square famous for its pop icons walking northward to the slopes of Hampstead and Highgate. I remember crossing once into the emerald shade of the famous cemetery and turning in dismay from Marx's tomb—the bronze bust evoking more the image of a misshapen old burgher than the thinker and revolutionary—to look for the grave, distinguished only by a modest stone obelisk, of Mary Ann Evans, author of *Middlemarch*.

Another day I went in the opposite direction: from St Mark's toward Maida Vale and Paddington, where red, green, and blue floating homes accompanied me at knee-level, and where sometimes the notes of a guitar or a friendly greeting rose up to meet me. Occasionally, I glimpsed in the dim interior of these houseboats stationary or moving figures busy with chores like it was the most natural thing in the world. Then, so as not to break the spell, I would look ahead and walk with care. This side of the canal was generally cooler, as if the richness of the white stucco terraces reflected in the trembling virescent waters had sucked the lingering warmth out of the air.

I would wait around Paddington for Rita to return from work and we would go to dinner by ourselves or with friends. Among them were several of our old classmates, using the study of law mostly as an excuse for having a good time. After what had long been endured at home, no one thought a year of graduate work abroad really onerous, not unless you harbored ambitions to top your class or join a big city firm or, more uncommonly, land a pupillage at a chamber. Even so, for those not particularly desperate, opportunities were opening up daily all over the city. Having availed themselves of the meager aid that colleges are wont to offer high fee-paying foreigners, these friends of ours had baited their solvent families to help bankroll their studies for three brief additional terms. Afterward, with the loop of allurement nicely closed, they floated from borough to borough in poor imitation of moneyed émigrés recently arrived in town—quick to take their pleasures and disappointments without paying much heed to either. Between a dull and grueling past and an indifferent future of passable wealth and mediocrity, it was a hiatus most dearly bought and arranged for.

For many of them this happy period was now nearing its end. Yet no one seemed especially perturbed. It was incredible to watch, this mad valor in the face of what lay ahead. Over slow meals in an East End bistro or a pub in Bayswater, once the day's job postings had been flippantly debated and dismissed, ideas were floated for trips to Italy, Greece, or the Costa Brava. In this our companions showed themselves to be not very original. I would look across the mess of sweating glasses and neglected dishes and find Rita listening with a show of interest to these impulsive, speculative schemes. A sort of tranquility radiated from her figure, the kind I hadn't seen since our first summer together, when, barely out of adolescence, the strength of our passions often took us by surprise. Soon, however, a signal ambition had impinged on this idyll, and six years of austerities had not been enough to attain it. Thrown back suddenly into those languid tropical nights, still heavy with the scent of frangipani blossoms in my memory, I wished for nothing more than to close the slight distance between us.

Prior to starting at Cambridge, Rita had firmed up her decision to live and work in London subsequently. In the very first week of classes, she was successful in securing ahead of time a training contract at a top city firm. Arriving hard on the heels of a generous scholarship, the news had amazed even her for once. In just a short period, life had resolved most of her pressing concerns, smoothing the way to a stable career. At the end of the two-year training, if things went per plan, she would be admitted as a solicitor on the rolls of the law society and be solidly on track to joining the English middle class. I suppose in her naïveté she believed to have hit upon an escape route from the general malevolence of the world.

When I noticed her feign interest over dinner that evening, she was all of twenty-three and about to enter her second six-month rotation at work. Young and circumspect in her hopes and yearnings, she was finding it hard to suppress her delight at such perfect unfolding of events. It was touching to watch her mutely struggle like this, amid people distracted by other, more fleeting emotions.

Too soon or too late, I had in the meantime come to feel the full weight of my choices, the sheer insanity of a life spent practicing law. In the early months on the job, lifting my bleary eyes from the drab papers and code books, I would stare at the gathering darkness in the window and wonder whose cause precisely did this vast textual edifice serve. Later, watching big corporations grow bigger by doing little else than follow the rules meant to keep them in check, I would have my answer. Small businesses, burdened by regulatory costs and slimming margins, were in due course outpaced and acquired by others with deeper pockets. And by helping the latter tap into markets at home and abroad, we also did our bit to deepen those pockets in the first place. When in this manner just a few players came to dominate a field, separate set of regulations could always be invoked to break monopolies and punish the more ambitious of the lot. It was dull, methodical, cyclical work which, if you dared to look past the handsome fees, made no sense at all.

Could John Locke and Robert Nozick be right? Was a minimal state the answer to my nocturnal agonies? Fewer laws to parse and more time to do as one pleased! Going against my own professional instincts, I would then feel a surge of sympathy for the libertarians, who appeared to my tormented soul as scattered orphans of some failed revolution. Mightn't they have saved us from this slow atrophy of the senses? The question seemed at least worth posing. But how exactly in such a cut-throat, laissez-faire, atavistic universe, if it had perchance come to pass, would I have indulged a talent that had few takers to begin with?

A mistake; a careless trespass into the wrong category. Lawyers, after all, are more positivists than philosophers by training.

'You are firmly on the road to ruin,' Rita would say to me light-heartedly in college. To succeed one had only to move logically along well-trodden paths and stay clear of the dangers of idealism. Now that life was proceeding beautifully, I imagined her thinking in private moments, why had this old nuisance reared its head to spoil the fun? During a performance at the Barbican, for which she had received complimentary tickets at work, or in her Finchley Road flat, whose windows narrowly framed the brisk English skies against the blue smoke of the gentians on the sill, I could sense her disquiet prick me across straightened silences.

How much longer could I saunter on like this? Seasonal pleasure trips stolen from the horrors of the court or the boardroom. I was simply delaying the inevitable. The easy solution was to admit the mistakes of the past and change course: to state openly that it was time to take Defoe and Kafka seriously for their own sake, to submit to a different function of the word. Not the heavy formalized legalese with its punctuated threats of sanction, but the swift, lively registers whose inner dialogism enlivened the mind and drew one to the very edge of thought.

(Oh, to put those dear to you on notice for such a trifle!)

Easy solution, I say? Easy and romantic and foolish. To my legal work I had taken a literary attitude, and it had bestowed on me the breezy confidence of the outsider, one who felt he had hardly any skin in the game. Like a traveler just starting out and hitching a ride up to the fork in the road, I discharged my duties with a sense of detachment and contingency. My rigor rarely, if ever, matched that of my colleagues. The firm was boutique and new, a breakaway from a larger practice. It was top heavy with several of the seniors having been broken early in their careers on the cogs of white-shoe behemoths in New York. When in the course of a cross-border deal or stock offering, the head partner invited the rare visiting lawyer from Cravath or Wachtell to our mahogany-rich, wainscoted premises, their slightest praise would make his sleep deprived eyes sparkle. Afterward, in high spirits, he avowed that his aim was to make our small firm the Wachtell of Asia. The boast, clearly unachievable, nonetheless had me worried. It meant longer nights and expanded misery. It meant being thrown into the deep end of the pool and learning to swim or sinking to the bottom unaided. That was the famous foreign model. It could easily overwhelm the most tenacious of the lot.

Wachtell. Lipton. Rosen. Katz. The leader in the blue suit gave a brief pause after each name to mark its Wall Street prestige. The firm was at the very top of the pecking order in New York, and New York, as everyone knew, possessed the deepest, most sophisticated financial markets in the world. Some more of his rehearsed words seeped through the static in my head. It looked as though he was reminiscing his years of drudgery and indulgence in America and wanted nothing more in middle age than to recreate at home, if feebly, the peculiar raptures of his youth.

But what had been achieved by four bright Jewish minds in the Manhattan of the Sixties, was not easy to replicate in the new millennium thousands of miles away. Born in the Depression era and shaped by its ethos, these men seemed to have carried from the start a sense of fair play and a wish to fight for the underdog, a sentiment quite beside the point by the time I went to work for the firm in Delhi. While we might have used in some of our commercial covenants and protocols a version or another of Martin Lipton's *poison pill* defense—a strategy designed to repel hostile takeover bids, and which had brought upon its author the ire of no less a figure than Milton Friedman—our concerns were usually not so lofty, the goal in near term always to work longer hours for more profits.

In this high-class, pushy environment, it was a matter of perpetual astonishment to me that my less than total determination was viewed with circumspection and indulgence; my love of literature with a certain cosy respect. Did these hardened, calculating minds also recognize some other power of the written word? Had they too in their youth dabbled in literature before relenting under pressure of one or another kind? And were they now tacitly egging me on to see if I would succeed where they had failed?

'Why not move to London? The place is practically bursting with offers.' The refrain followed me everywhere during that second summer in England. From our common friends, from her work colleagues, from Rita herself, I kept hearing variants of the same question.

'If only you'd tried harder last year,' Rita sighed, watching a group our age shrieking with delight and playing ball in Hyde Park the evening prior to my departure. I saw no point in repeating what she knew already, but I said it anyway.

She was suddenly impatient and acerbic. Uncertainty, a vague fear of the unknown, was her Achilles' heel. In her features there was now a visible harshness. Uncertainty, ambiguity, negative capability. Keats though won't have been much of a comfort just then. 'This will end in tears of blood,' I thought tritely but didn't say to her.

The previous September Rita had come across an opening for a role similar to hers at another member of the Magic Circle set. She had wanted me to apply. I wasn't so confident. The sole opening was outside the firm's yearly hiring cycle. Possibly, they had someone specific in mind. I didn't see myself fitting the bill. 'Why,' I reasoned, 'should they take an outsider when there are thousands of perfectly capable locals to choose from?'

Buoyed up perhaps by her own lucky circumstances, Rita had brushed aside my objections and had been proven right, up to a point, by subsequent events. I cleared the preliminary tests and assignments without much difficulty and was invited to London at the firm's expense for further sessions and interviews. The news came as a surprise, yet I was ambivalent, not entirely convinced of my desires or of their seriousness to hire me.

But the truth was that recent developments in trade and technology had opened up the world and made the large English firms ambitious. They were in a hurry to grow their footprint in Asia ahead of their American peers. Although local laws barred foreign practices from operating on Indian soil, many were already active in our markets through offices in London, Singapore, and Hong Kong. On the side, these firms quietly lobbied for the removal of any such barriers to entry. Deep down they saw it as inevitable: the flooding of the dykes by the gathering tide of global finance. They wanted to be ready when this happened. Young lawyers like me fitted their future needs perfectly.

I reached London early and went straight to the place on Great Portland Street where I had a booking. Due to a slip-up in schedule, no single room was vacant until noon next day. Instead, I was shown a kind of dormitory with three prior occupants: a Chilean father and son and, as if to set them in contrast, a tall blonde Canadian in rude health. The Chileans were poor; the father had the smile of a new immigrant, valiant and easy yet unable to mask the confusion of arrival, of having reached a place from which there now seemed no escape possible, while the Canadian Apollo felt only the minor discomfort of unmet expectations. He was in the mother country on a short working holiday and there was a chiding note in his voice. He spoke of the narrow streets and dwellings, of the crowds at dusk and the dinginess of stations at night. He looked at the boy, small and silent, then asked the father if he didn't want to come along to pick something to eat from the discount shelves at the supermarket. But father and son had received their meals earlier in church and needed nothing more for the day. The Canadian left, and soon a dreamy stillness settled upon the air.

I thought of stretching in bed for a bit. When I woke up, the Chilean was busy making coffee from a sachet. He saw me rise and pushed the boy in my direction. In his little hands was a half-filled paper cup. Poor and exposed they may have been, but the two still carried their courtesies with them. I felt strange and ridiculous. I didn't understand what I was doing in England.

Two days later, the absurd had fully entered me. I can't say I minded the intrusion. A part of me might even have welcomed the trade-off. It loosened the shackles of ambition and injected a sense of play into the world, restoring things and feelings to their proper measure. So, on the rush hour Tube to Canary Wharf, it was possible to shake off the outsider's nerves and act out instead the homely angst of the citizen being whisked away via hidden routes to the site of his quotidian suffering.

The new swanky building grew in the transparent arch of the station exit as I rode the escalator up to street level. The morning was windy and overcast. I lingered on the sidewalk directly across the imposing entrance to prepare a face for the long crucial appointment. The old stony messiness of the City had here been exchanged for a certain mathematical symmetry and openness: a latter-day glass enclave erected hurriedly in the crook of the Thames that spoke of new money and whose airy cleanliness was subtly oppressive. Behind me in the carefully laid-out gardens, the paths winding along trimmed hedges and plashing fountains were quickened by the steps of officegoers in sharp suits, while away on the greensward, young mothers cooed to their newborns under short ornamental trees with shiny leaves. This was still the Isle of Dogs and Greenwich lay just beyond the slow curl of the river, but on that distant morning the entire place exuded an aura of the make believe.

A cyclist entered my vision, parked the bike on the stand next to the entrance and, smoothing his suit with both hands, breezed into the building. I felt it was time I too tasted the magic of this charmed circle.

I joined a dozen other candidates waiting in the expensive lobby. We soon found ourselves in a meeting room whose outer glass wall framed the Millennium Dome in a clutch of leaden water. My peers adapted to the place quickly. Nobody looked out; some were even reaching for the tea and sandwich trays in the corner. Then the group sessions began.

In my team was a clever boy from Oxford. Wavy hair, gray pinstriped suit, and all the correct answers delivered in that snug accent. Mentally, I handed him the job after just a few minutes. It took off the pressure and helped my performance. At lunch, I chatted with a girl from Durham who was no less impressive. Talent, proper accents, a complete homogeneity of education and experience. So much to choose from right under your nose, and yet, the firm had offered a misfit like me a seat at the table. The gesture spoke of my evolving luck amid the changing signs of the world.

One of the partners I hadn't seen before drifted over to us. I let the Durham girl engage her as I stole a glance to confirm that the Dome was still standing after all those hours of testing. The woman saw me looking out and asked if I had any plans before my flight back home. I had nothing interesting to say, so I made it up: 'Leaving for Cornwall tomorrow. St Ives.' And as she expressed her appreciation and made further inquiries, the trip began to take shape in my head.

'Barbara Hepworth(?)' the Durham girl hid her ignorance well behind a careful absence of inflection. The woman did better. Clearly, she knew of Hepworth. Maybe she even owned one of her early sculptures. She pressed me further, and the phenomenological impulse I had suppressed until then flared up easily. I said something about form, resonance, and the textured throbbing of matter. Words of a Rilke poem came to me: *what skies are reflected in the inland lake of these roses.* I offered them to her as such. In the eyes of the girl from Durham, I now saw a suspicion confirmed. The partner, on the other hand, couldn't hold back her smile. She wished us luck for the final interview and moved on.

An hour later, I met her again in a room higher up in the building. At first, she calmly watched a fellow colleague grill me over regulatory issues in a merger deal. When she saw that I was beginning to repeat myself, she nudged the discussion in her own area of practice. I knew less about Debt than Equities; about Structured Finance and Derivatives I frankly knew very little. She came straight to the point and said in her soft reassuring voice: 'Could you talk a bit on Collateralized Debt Obligations?' To speak slightly on an entire technical branch of commercial lending and investment! She had me trapped. The casual generality of the question was meant to test not my knowledge but the extent of my comfort in the field.

By this time, CDOs had become the pet gambling product of Wall Street. Whatever their provenance, they were then being used principally as instruments which dressed up and securitized toxic debt that no one wanted to touch. Employing abstract mathematical models devoid of any reality, the New York banks had learned to repackage and sell these loans to institutional investors chasing yields in a low rate environment. Early successes of the experiment were replicated with alacrity across Europe and Asia. The math was complicated, and in truth nobody could have assessed the value of the underlying debt correctly. But when everyone is winning, it is in bad taste to show concern. Because financial institutions could now pass off these loans to willing investors, it freed up their books and incentivized them to advance new credit. Low-quality debt carried bigger risks and yielded higher returns, therefore, by a perfect inversion of logic and common sense those with lower creditworthiness came to be preferred to the more stable earners. Before long the world had been fully turned on its head, and instruments that bet on the underlying debt defaulting were being floated and bought at auctions in the thousands.

In a way, CDOs were the perfect culmination of an era of financial engineering that America had unleashed on the world since the end of the Cold War. For the entirety of this period, Alan Greenspan had been the Chairman of the Federal Reserve Board. Presidents came and went, but Chairman Greenspan hung on in the Eccles Building, repeatedly professing the freedom of markets in the face of calls to tame their excesses, yet not hesitating himself to undermine that same freedom by artificially supressing rates in order to keep the appetite for risk high and the addiction to cheap money going.

This easy availability of debt—an accounting trick, a play of numbers really—came at the cost of productivity and left behind over time diminishing returns and an ever-widening wealth gap. Years later when Rita and I arrived in America to start a new life, the disastrous social and political consequences of what had begun in the Nineties were all around us.

I knew hardly any of this on the day of my interview. I was too young and self-obsessed to care, lacking in experience necessary to join the dots in the constellation of international finance. I filled in the details only later, alongside the rest of the world, by when the seasoned hands had long since cashed in their chips and exited the burning casino.

But had I known the facts could I have simply offered them to my questioner? More knowledge in this case would have been hazardous. Few there cared about the larger ramifications of such products; in fact, the firm's core interests were perfectly aligned with those of its clients that created and traded them daily. The partner merely wanted to see if I was capable enough to work the code that made these things look legal. Evidently, my words failed to satisfy her. I tried to bury my misery in the lone ray of light entering the carafe of orange juice by the window. Debt; liquidity; the velocity of money. These were the levers that moved the world. Such grand ideas about Hepworth and Rilke (whoever he might be), she must have said to herself, and so little knowledge of the things that lent the earth its extra spin.

'The place is practically bursting with offers,' the girl in the cream silk top had spoken over the noisy chatter of the pub. But I didn't need her to tell me, I could see it myself everywhere. Behind the easy laughter of friends and strangers, behind the mania for nightlong parties and rushed trips to the Continent, I thought I heard the muffled echoes of the Jazz Age. Same gaiety; less hauteur. Anyone who didn't experience that absurd and happy period in their prime could have scarcely understood the sentiment. As if the Roaring Twenties were back, financially engineered and brought forward to mark the new millennium. The energy and optimism that summer in London—the affluence I brushed against here and there—were altogether different in scale from what I had seen or read about until then. And fired up by the near daily boasts of Chancellor Brown, who aimed to put London ahead of New York as the go-to place for raising large sums quickly, the city papers fueled the euphoria still further.

Its scale may have seemed different, but in truth the optimism was just skin-deep, tenuous, encased like the air inside a bubble. And the bubble was real, fed by cheap money and synthetic instruments like CDOs. Of course, these weren't the only American imports. The New Labour of Tony Blair and Gordon Brown had carefully followed the lead of Bill Clinton in reviving the Democratic Party and had come away with important lessons on how to put the political economy in the service of one's own ambition.

The borrowed idea, practical sounding if potentially dangerous, was to harness the power of markets in furthering the public good. The scheme must have pleased Chairman Greenspan in Washington, for it seemed straight out of his own playbook. But England was not America; its economy at the time was a fraction of the latter. To make the plan work, therefore, it was imperative to look out just when America was looking in: to steal a march on the hegemon while it was smarting from the attack on the Twin Towers and the messy unfolding of the Enron scandal; to quickly unshackle the financial sphere and channel as much global capital flows through the City's trading exchanges as was possible; and to finally have the resilience and good sense to not interfere when the money ran wild and brought the speculators in.

It was in this environment of rising profits and spreading risks that Rita had gone to work for the firm in London and that I had been called to the interview in Canary Wharf. By next summer, when I had taken my walks along the canal lined with narrowboats, going one day in the direction of Hampstead and Highgate, and on another toward Maida Vale and Paddington, the mood had been merrier, the offers numerous, the pay more lucrative. Yet it made little sense to pick up here the burden I was planning to drop elsewhere.

I had tried once and failed. And the failure had saved me. I knew enough stories of people arriving in the great metropolis and slowly going to seed in the mill of relentless misery and boredom to not act otherwise. Plus, what was coming out of the presses of London didn't exactly inspire you to be near them: prose lacking in all mystery, so watery you could have stared right through it at the chintz curtains lining the author's study. The other kind of writing, the one full of grit and passion, and which seldom made into print, needed experiences I did not possess. But one doesn't go looking for such experiences. When your luck runs out, you get them aplenty. What emerges later, pleasing though it may be for the reader, is desperate and reductive: openness of vision isn't a quality you develop moving beer pints around a taproom.

Both extremes horrified me. To look for the golden mean was to act alone. And to act alone it was first necessary to not abandon the familiar.

To my legal work I had taken a literary attitude, but to literature itself I could only bring my inexperience and a portmanteau of bookish tricks. And why shouldn't one city be as good for producing pastiche as another? Whether you were accepted into this or that clique was irrelevant if you had only the weekends to fulfil a passion or break a fever. That was the line of Rita's reasoning. It was both correct and beside the point. It got us nowhere.

By the next winter, the world had gone to hell.

Then a day before my departure for America, my legs, as if from some dormant instinct, had hit upon the route of my youth again. I was suddenly seized by the wish to cross Regent's Park and go up to St Mark's at the corner of Primrose Hill and see once more, after a period of twelve years, those pretty boats stretching on either side from the bend in the canal. But my step had lost its swiftness—the world its illusions—and by the time I felt the first cobbles of Fitzroy Square underfoot I had changed my mind. Flanked by those stuccoed Georgian terraces, I took to one of the benches facing the round fenced-in garden over which the old plane trees like so many wellsprings were casting their cool lushness at that hour. Close by on Great Portland Street was the establishment where I had met the poor courteous Chileans long ago. What had become of the father and son in the intervening decade that had been so harsh on so many?

Traveling to London in the Spring of 1822 amid all the pomp and deference due to the newly appointed Ambassador of Louis XVIII to the English Court, the now middle-aged Vicomte de Chateaubriand remembered a young François-René, who having been wounded at Thionville had reached the port of Southampton via Jersey in May 1793 and, poor and sick, had made his way to this same city under very different circumstances. On both those occasions, Chateaubriand had lived not far from the square where I was now sitting, and, like myself, had the second time around gone walking the familiar streets in search of old sights and faces. In his famous memoirs, he writes with feeling and only a slight exaggeration of gladly leaving his handsome carriage at the corner of this or that square and losing himself in the back alleys he had frequented during the destitute days of his youth. An entire colony of French émigrés fleeing the turbulence of wars and revolutions had settled in this part of London, and it was here that he had nursed himself back to health on the bread and charity of strangers and finally completed the romances that were later to make him famous. In those bygone days, Chateaubriand recalled, he often lacked the money to buy paper and was forced to fasten the scribbled sheets with tacks pulled from the windowsill of his garret, a narrow inhospitable space that he shared with another brother in suffering for six shillings a month.

On such solitary walks at the beginning of his embassy in London, overcome with nostalgia, Chateaubriand noted the great change that had come to the place. The surrounding open country of three decades earlier had given way to lavish homes, wide avenues, bridges and promenades. Large meadows dotted with herds of cattle that were once visible from his humble dwelling had vanished without a trace into the orderly beauty of Regent's Park. New sights, lamented the ageing viscount, had encroached upon the fading memories of past events, and a whole epoch filled with the tears and happiness of youth had quietly slipped into their shadow.

For the moments I had been reminded of Chateaubriand and his strange destiny, the many glories and tragedies of his life, the difficult journeys he had undertaken to witness the birth of nations and the fall of empires, not a sound could be heard on that distinguished square. No one passed through any of the arched doorways, no footfall echoed on the sidewalk, no birdsong or the clap of a wingbeat reached me.

'One inhabits, with a full heart, an empty world.' Chateaubriand's credo that had inspired a generation of artists and romantics had lately been much on my mind, although in my present state, and to show me the slow decline of my own creative tendencies, the obverse seemed to echo the truth better: the heart empty and the world full.

To shake off this feeling perhaps, I had taken Rita out of London all the way to the North Lakes. Midway in Derbyshire, we stayed on a farm at the bottom of a valley that you reached driving through pinched country lanes with homes flushed with the road. There were horses in the stables and, in the old stone cottage, a German Boxer bitch that took an extreme liking to Rita, barely leaving her side, waking her up in the morning, and settling beneath the long bathroom windows while she took a shower. Hiking uphill at noon, one saw coppices of hornbeam, oak, and mountain ash scattered through fields and pastures under stippled light and, at the end of a row of conifers over the ridgeline, entered a desolate moor capped by sudden low skies. Later, crossing a three-arched bridge over River Derwent, we toured a manor house serene in its misty web of parklands and wooded hills. *Lovely as an unenraged mind*, I remembered a line from Les Murray just as a weak Midland sun slipped free of clouds and broke into gold on its baroque walls. The next day somewhere between Manchester and Kendal rain finally overtook us. Driving through sheets of water, it occurred to me that perhaps it was near here two centuries earlier that the writer and opium addict Thomas De Quincey had experienced his own mortality in a shiver-vision of death atop the nightly mail coach. From Kendal to Grasmere to Keswick, along the bank of one lake or another, it was De Quincey not Coleridge or Wordsworth who had been my guide. And it was through the prism of his words mainly that I had witnessed the birthplace of English Romanticism.

But among the meres and fells of Cumbria, the solitude was the solitude of stones at the bottom of those moody trembling bodies of water, weighty and mysterious. Even the light, soft, numinous, stretching the vision over vast distances, had the feel of this solitude. It did little for the hollow and wizened heart, except to serve a reminder of its poverty amid the numberless riches of the world.

Swift are the chariots of mind! Scarcely a quarter of an hour had passed since I had left Gramercy Park behind and made my way west on Twentieth. And yet, already I had filled a couple of unfamiliar blocks with two decades of memories, resurrected suddenly by the simple sight of an enclosed private space. Speeding past the byways of lost years, I ended up dilating the present. On Broadway, my roving thoughts at last caught up with my steps. The city's loud scream threading innumerable ravines entered and coursed through my blood. Clouds that I had seen above the open country from my airport taxi now covered from end to end the once lofty skies of Manhattan.

On the plaza outside Madison Square Park where Broadway intersects Fifth Avenue, a middle-aged man in a red cap was selling touristy photos and artwork. Reading the evening paper in a collapsible chair, he looked clearly unenthused about the entire proposition. Not troubling himself to collect the small bills offered in payment every now and then, he merely pointed to the tin can at the end of the table. His composure, that complete indifference to money in such a setting, was interesting to follow. Could one survive on so little in this capital of high finance, this expensive metropolis of fashion and culture? To his left, and providing a study in contrast, rose the pointy façade of the Flatiron Building, cleaving the wave of traffic, as the old simile went, like the prow of a ship moving up the harbor. Like a wedge, it seemed to secure the lower to the upper half of the island.

Only moments ago, I had passed its entire stretch along Broadway. But from the side at street level the building was just a row of storefront windows separated by blocks of limestone. For the entire drama of its eclectic, revivalist style—the double columns, the terracotta embellishments and simulated rustications, the heavy running cornice—was projected into its angular front. Built at the end of the Gilded Age and one of its last functioning remnants, the kind that brought to mind the old New York of Edith Wharton and Henry James, the Flatiron aroused a feeling of muted wonder among its more modern, showy neighbors.

Inside the park, the dark had come, and little girls were chasing fireflies on the grass. Above the trees, the loggia of the Met Life Tower released a beautiful saffron glow that netted the Venetian green of the dormers and the gold of the cupola. I walked some further blocks north and ended up eating a light meal at a Korean joint. Then I took a taxi back to the room. It had started to rain.

Form, as Hobbes knew, is power, and in New York, this power had reached a crescendo during the Jazz Age. Three hundred years after the Dutch had asserted their claim on the tip of Manhattan, the city was ready to molt its European skin and grow a soul. In the nightclubs of Harlem, the new tunes of Duke Ellington and Johnny Hodges, and amid the rush of faces on the West Side, flashing visions of King Oliver and Louis Armstrong, Sidney Bechet and Mamie Smith. Meanwhile, on the other side of Central Park, the stepped towers, shorn of the age-old revivalist and Beaux-Arts urges, and as if anticipating the long economic depression round the corner, rose with incredible urgency higher and higher into the ashen vortex of the sky.

Like with music, fresh discoveries in architecture had come to the North East, somewhat surprisingly, from the interior of the country. Technological innovations in construction materials that had previously been tested in Paris and Vienna, first attained austere and vertical manners in certain structures of the Midwest. In the Manhattan of the late Twenties, these manners evolved into a distinct grammar of style. The island's peculiar topography and grid plan, coupled with a new zoning law which prescribed setbacks for tall buildings to ensure ample light for the streets below, gave rise to some of the most recognizable skyscrapers of the modern era. Their solid, simplified, zigguratish appearance—quieter ornamentation, strong vertical lines with successively telescoping levels, the geometric patterning and abstract bas-relief—wasn't universally admired at the time and was often half-pejoratively referred to as being in the 'modern' or 'vertical' style. Not until the Sixties, when gazing past the dreariness of much of the post-war architecture cluttering the city's skyline, did a true appreciation of the artistic grandeur of these buildings begin to take shape in the collective imaginary. *Arts Décoratifs*, from the famous interwar exhibition in Paris, became simply *Art Deco*, and the catchy name, fitting the appearance, had stuck and matured.

Sundry influences had coalesced to produce this look. If the outward form displayed the effects of Cubism, Expressionism, the Vienna Secession of the *Palais Stoclet* and *Majolica House*, then inside, striking murals celebrating new and emergent technologies of the day adorned the ceilings of ornate lobbies. The rich detailed interiors were frequently of an Aztec, African, or Eastern cast cleverly meshed with the decorative arts of Europe then much in vogue. A kind of latter-day *Gesamtkunstwerk* it was, conveying a holistic, quintessentially New World complexion amid the outmoded styles of an earlier epoch.

When the rain stopped at noon and the finches came out to sing in the tree under my balcony, I went in search of these tall glittering symbols of Deco New York.

Clouds swollen and gray trailed low over the city walls, and the streets once more were flooded with people. I rode the subway down to the Financial District, then thought of beginning even earlier and walked over to Tribeca to see the Woolworth Building. Modeled on the tower in the Westminster Palace and completed in the year 1912, its Gothic façade, accentuated by vertical window bays and glazed terracotta panels, already gave a whiff of Deco before its time. Then, too, the phonetic proximity of the terms was not without interest. For what was Deco anyway but that brooding, revivalist English impulse surprised and arrested by the spread of Modernism in the years following the Great War?

To retrace your steps shortly thereafter and come face to face with the Irving Trust Company Building at One Wall Street was to be granted something of a revelation. Here, all that had hitherto lain abstract and unclear in me regarding Modernism was made concrete in a flash of understanding. And while much that was once avant-garde in literature had faded into oblivion, this Ralph Walker designed Deco beauty continued to please the mind and the eye with its delicately achieved harmonies. The lancet windows at street level, clearly a homage to Trinity Church across Broadway, were set in gently angling limestone walls resembling a wave or a curtain. Those walls soared fifty stories to a crown ribbed and chevroned on every side like a flower drawn by Picasso.

Modernism: not the drama of unceasing thoughts and transitory, enigmatic visions, but the hard labor of hands and the sweet promise of progress. Put Whitman next to Baudelaire, suggested Franco Moretti, and the picture at once got clearer. 'Years of the modern!' sang Whitman, 'years of the unperform'd!'

To understand Modernism in this way was in fact to understand the allure of America. For the modern sensibility had ripened like fruit from the tree of capital, and America, if nothing else, had been from the moment of its founding openly capitalist. This causality had encountered in architecture a perfect ally and had created subsequently the towering pinnacles of the movement. My knowledge, gleaned from the literatures of Europe, which had increasingly spoken to my own early distaste for the financial world's slavish, mechanistic tendencies, had deliberately sidelined this facet of Modernism: that it was as much a techno-scientific revolution as a humanistic one. This partial blanking out was helpful however: it gave me the freedom to take sides and act quickly, make mistakes and move on. Credit also had to be given to the genius of European artists and thinkers, many of whom themselves heirs to a declining aristocracy, for having forged from the still smoldering ruins of Romantic thought a loud new consciousness and language of dissent. It was supremely attractive to young people everywhere, and its appeal had diminished but slightly over the century. That the rallying cry for the group had come from an expat American sustained by the money and confidence of the New World was of course only mildly ironic and could easily be overlooked.

So perhaps it was here then, observing this part gothic, part cubist, part deconstructionist jewel of the Jazz Age, standing tall at the juncture of two synecdochical streets, that I unknowingly started to acclimate to America.

After Ralph Walker, Raymond Hood. This Twenties' bad boy of architecture had fully outgrown his previous persona by the time he came to reign over Midtown as its most sought-after Deco planner. One look at the austere façade of the Rockefeller Center and you saw right away that Hood unlike Walker was least interested in establishing any harmonies whatsoever with the older style of the famous cathedral across the road. If a little earlier, his American Radiator Building had made me entertain fleeting thoughts of Cologne Cathedral, it wasn't due to anything in its form per se, which had the trademark straight lines and flat surfaces of the new movement, but because the massing, soot-stained with gilt edges, conveyed the feel of a medieval monument encased in a modern shell, strangely unsettling against the low heavens, unworldly in a somber, Lovecraftian sort of way.

Later, lying in bed in the airconditioned quiet of the night, unable to fall asleep, I went to work on the day's impressions. They took me back to my mechanical drawing classes in school: my clean draughtsmanship, the joy of copying building plans and machine blocks on large cartridge sheets clipped to the board, my early success among my peers. Through the rolling weekly sessions, a play of forms under the sliding T-square, and sometimes in the silence of things, the fading echo of cricket practice in the nets or the sweet laughter of girls creeping up the wall—a surge of emotion in the small hours once, and the slow unraveling of a dream.

Long ago my wish had been to create on a grand scale one day, measuring and transforming the world of things. Instead, I'd ended up on the other side of the spectrum. Form not as power but as mode of survival. Not heady and vertiginous, but tactile, subtle: expanding life from the inside, teaching humility daily. Personality indeed had become fate.

Beyond the cone of lamplight, there suddenly shimmered in the abstract print above the sofa, Georgia O'Keeffe's depiction of the Radiator Building by night. Reds, yellows, and whites speckled across gray rectilinear blocks; streetlamps floating like bubbles and blue rotating beams, greened along the edges by chimney smoke, roughening the city air. A lone star in one corner, the easy to miss sign of O'Keeffe's mystical brilliance, putting all that human fussiness in perspective. And, finally, the tall black bulk in the foreground, aglow with rectangular windows, rising to a ram's head with horns curving away and dissolving in my sleep.

From Brooklyn to Washington Heights, Deco had risen like a tidal wave in the soul of New York. It had left behind countless big and small treasures that out of their web of significations continued to gladden the heart to this date. Together, they made up the great loom on which the city's aura had been woven, patterned, and thickened over time. But if Deco was the defining motif of the Jazz Age, then one structure before all else symbolized its lofty and magnetic pull right into the present moment. This, of course, was the Chrysler Building.

'A Rhapsody in Chrome,' an old article in the *Times* had called it, evoking for the reader not only the lingering edginess of jazz but also the euphoric rush of the Twenties. For me, the building's unmistakable presence on the skyline—that ribbed and shiny multi-arched crown tapering to a slender steel spire—had forever been synonymous with New York. It was the one thing I most wanted to see. And, in fact, I had seen it straight away from a distance on my walk along Irving Place the evening of my arrival. Those gleaming Byzantine arches, each tiered setback filled with vaulted triangular windows and sunbursts, were a clear reminder of William Van Alen's Beaux-Arts training in Paris, his solitary courage and distinctive genius. While his peers were jettisoning revivalist designs for flat tops and surfaces, Van Alen had been so bold as to defamiliarize the past and offer it as new. He had mixed curves and angles in a style reminiscent of a temple in the East thereby opening himself to charges of exhibitionism and empty eclecticism. Neither traditional, the critics had objected, nor properly modern! But the *Chrysler* had survived the dialectics of history. Its crown never failed to send a mysterious thrill through me whenever the building showed itself amid the packed chessboard of Manhattan.

High up from a neighboring tower, I once saw that stepped roof diagonally at eye level. The steel curves reflecting late light over the glowing tubes in the windows were a frozen firework celebration in the sky.

I had read somewhere that Goethe on his journey through Italy had stood before a Palladian villa and calmed the raging passions in his soul. Inspired, he had begun his *Iphigenia* in a hurry. Would the *Chrysler* do for me what Andrea Palladio's architectural harmonies had once done for Goethe? Will my long creative drought end some day and the clogged springs freshen and flow again?

The final afternoon of my stay was spent in the company of old masters at *The Frick*. When I came out, the trees bordering the park had the look of rain in them and the lights along the avenue were wet and smudgy. In the plaza, the slight breeze spoke of horses and exhaust fumes. The sky was clearing now, and the glow from high terraces was beginning to pass through it. Less busy than others, certain streets still held brief misty patches in their shadow depths, while small pedestrian clusters at every crossing were like last week's clotted snow.

George Coleman was performing at Jazz Standard that evening. How easy it seemed, to walk a few blocks, descend some stairs, and settle down in the company of legends. *My Horns of Plenty!* Coleman's fast vibrato, his licks and melodies, brought forth fitful memories of listening to him during my long-gone law days. I hadn't followed jazz much over the years; soon Coleman was flying, and I couldn't keep up with him. Giving him company, closing the gaps left by his tenor saxophone, was Coleman's friend and post-bop pianist Harold Mabern, who played the thing throughout like a boss.

Coleman Jr.'s brushes got entangled in the wheels of my rail car. The train, mutating distance into time, was swiftly pushing New York into the past. But the slow churn it had wrought in me was bound to seed and bear fruit.

For once, the sun shone bright over the entire valley. Scarcely a decade after the Revolutionary War, François-René de Chateaubriand had sailed this very stretch of the Hudson in a packet boat to Albany. His aim was to move up quickly and steadily through the wildernesses of Niagara and Canada—a silly, ill-prepared, ruse of a quest to discover the North-West Passage just when political turbulence back home was tightening its grip on his family. What distractions amid this endless verdure had eased the soul of the young viscount on that distant evening?

At level with the river, inside it, there came in view a floating forest, and beyond, on the other bank, more woods rising in tiers, clouds scraping their tops and trailing between heights.

The water here was still and deep, a bit marshy on the edges. After months and years, I found myself easing up a little. The train was coasting along the valley floor as if the pressure of the universe was non-existent. My vision became free of limits; my thoughts turned lofty.

'You won't be far from her,' Herman had said taking my leave. 'I'll come when I can.'

'And once together,' I tried to indulge him, 'will we join the pieces and watch the crags lift the crumbling monasteries back into the sky?' Will the leopards and streams be there still, the thought arose in the wake of my own voice, quickening that cold, bare plateau with the brittle charms of youth?

As if he could see her now, as if the years had had no purchase on her, Herman spoke of Rosamund climbing the narrow twisty track above the village at noon, rocks and wildflowers at her knee. Over his shoulder, I caught a glimpse of Rita and Niki coming down the steps, whispering conspiratorially like schoolgirls.

II

Fathers and sons. Fraying bonds in the wintry tide. The dawn mists low over the river, hanging tentative like a half-visited dread. A blast of horns in the gray air, their notes pressing firm against the chest. Dim golden echoes beneath heavy nebulous words too late to voice.

Right through my childhood, my father had carried something of the romantic in him. He was in his thirties before I was three: a mid-level public servant in the sluggish capital not two score years since the end of the Raj. For the boy who'd swum the fast icy stream to the village school each morning—for the boy still alive in him somewhere—a little of the romance was now renewed daily as he passed the lush boulevards and rotaries en route the main secretariat building on the hill. How absurd those large imperialist Beaux-Artsy structures in summer's harsh light; how sad the pigeon-flaked, red-stoned fountains steaming away in their chipped symmetries, when slummy colonies proliferating right outside this enclave of colonnades and bungalows had made plain the stasis and meanness of centuries of plunder.

The monochromatic solitude of days and the dull molecular constancy of work, a certain socialist languor that slowed all progress, evening conversations in smoky deteriorating coffeehouses where the fare was passable and the old British rituals still intact, the swift implicit terror of birds at dusk—this too was part of the charm of the time. My father had married my mother, the eldest of five daughters, from a family straight out of Jane Austen, full of bonhomie and warm-hearted simplicity, neither rich nor poor. Did he ever pause to consider the coincidence, given how much he admired Austen? I doubt it. For while he was descended from landed gentry himself and there had been money, a lot of it, only a generation or two earlier, his own upbringing, and that of his siblings after him, had been fairly modest. He could never have seen himself as coming from privilege.

In his boyhood, I'd heard tell, my grandfather had regularly accompanied his older brother on tours of the family estates and granaries, partly to distract himself and partly to learn and prepare for life. On such trips, the new brougham was brought out and, once the day's business was done, the siblings would call on relatives in nearby villages. Next day, the entire pack of cousins, seven or eight adolescent boys and girls, went picnicking in a remote meadow cradled by sheer cliffs of rock and ice at whose feet the thick pine forests abruptly ended, and where at dusk the shepherds welcomed them into their camp and fed them mutton stew by firelight. The cinders floated above the crackling logs and the sight was slowly lifted toward galaxies that hummed and arced in a widening river of milk and fell through snow peaks barely an arm's length away.

But the fairy tale had ended badly. And little more than a fairy tale it seemed whenever I tried to piece together the story of the misfortune that, swift as lightning, had struck my grandfather's family: the magnificent house amidst the charming scenery that had roused the envy of a passing prince, the great fire in the barns and outbuildings soon after, claims and lawsuits, financial ruin. Like a pastoral romance from a different century, like a chronicle people told in the old days to pass the time, the speedy logic of its events both banal and coherent, its few ambiguous lessons leaving no residue, dissolving into the black sky. Almost overnight, the world my grandfather had known had ceased to be. And for the new world in which he found himself he was thoroughly unprepared and useless. It seemed dreadful and incomprehensible, and, bit by bit, it had stymied him.

To my child's imagination, as my father pointed that meadow out to me one afternoon in the village, it was scarcely believable. I was collecting pebbles by the stream behind our cottage when, stopping by, he whimsically began to speak of his hiking trips there just like his father's had been in his own time. A verdant spot touched by late light against a background of winding glacial fields, the reds and yellows hardly visible from this distance, the whole thing hanging at the edge of words or vision (I knew not which), and about to be swallowed up by clouds rising from the evergreens below.

Small and quick like a cat I was at that time. So in the main family home next to the cottage that my uncles had vacated for us, in the twilight hour when the last cackle of the geese had faded on the chill air, I snuggled into my grandfather's loose *pheran* and, careful not to put my hand in the hot kanger somewhere inside the cloak too, quizzed him about what I had been told earlier. Even then, merely a boy of four, I could see how luxurious his own trips had been compared to my father's. In any event, they fitted my fantasies of the place better, fantasies that continued to deepen while I was away in the city, but which were hurriedly smudged out when the paradise as I had found it for a few weeks, pristine and undisturbed, went up in flames and was lost for ever.

Dinner I often had in my grandmother's lap. She would kiss me every few minutes and whisper sweet nothings in a language I didn't understand. I can still see her slick, silvery hair parted in the middle over a pale forehead, the smooth delicate features and thin lips of a Russian doll, her quick affection and warm smile full of half rotten teeth. After her sudden death just nine years later, I came across in one of my father's books an old photograph of her as a young girl. Unmistakable that piercing gaze even in a child's countenance, engaging me from the sepia depths of the past. A small picture with the top left corner overexposed. My grandmother was dressed for sport, golf or polo I couldn't tell, on a field that my father believed to be somewhere in the Karakoram, a territory now across the *de facto* border. But for the severity of the eyes and the chin, there was scarcely anything to connect the child in the photo with the simple ageing woman I recalled from my holidays. The life of that girl seemed to belong to a wholly different order of things. To my grandmother in the winter of her years, that distant childhood must have appeared utterly sumptuous and dreamlike. What had fueled the decline in her status so early in life?

In his time, her father had been among a handful of engineers in the service of the British, a rare distinction affording both prestige and wealth, for the British not only controlled the subcontinent, they also held suzerainty over the vast mountainous princely state, which, lying in the knot of three of the greatest ranges on earth, was of extreme significance to their geopolitical interests in Asia. For a while, therefore, my grandmother's family had lived well in the lap of the Himalaya. Then one day the engineer left for an official survey near Hidden Peak and failed to return. His body could not be located. And just like that, in a short period of time, the mirage of bungalows and servants, the ease and luxury of life amid those elevations had ended. My great grandmother was still alive when my father took us back there for the holidays. I retain but faint visions of her, sitting in a corner by the wood-fired earthen stove, a sprinkling of freckles on her pink face, white plaited hair issuing from under the red embroidered silk cap (which subsequently came into my sister's possession), chain smoking and smiling beatifically. I do not remember her ever speaking to anyone. My mother later said she loved my father to bits.

So innocence had found innocence; misfortune, readily, had closed around misfortune. The errors of the world had driven my grandparents to one another, and they had settled into their new marital routine without complaint. Although their circumstances were much reduced from what either had known only some years previously, they were not entirely without means. Nonetheless, my father, their first child, had to grow up fast and do some growing up for them in the bargain. He barely had a chance to enjoy his childhood, a state of being that seemed to be reserved for other children in the household. For his time and setting though, he was quite precocious, and was loved and respected by both sides of the family. At nineteen, he was reading Tolstoy; at twenty, he had enough fortitude to get through a Moravia. He had patience and wisdom beyond his years and was generally quite forgiving by temperament—a quality, which as the years go by, I realize I have come to inherit from him.

Each year at the end of summer, my parents would arrange a few weeks' leave from work to spend time with my father's family. The night train departing Delhi went whistling through the fields of Punjab that shimmered in the carriage window like moonlit waves in a lagoon. Hardly a hut or building, marooned on its own dark isle, broke the view for long periods. At dawn, the train came to a halt beside an empty platform with the presence of steep hills in the layered fog. We transferred to a bus and went straight for them, the air from the pines cool around my temples as it rushed in the open window at every hairpin bend. The weather cleared; the plain fell away. I kept rolling in and out of sleep for much of the morning. Parallel ridges in diminishing pastel hues rose one behind the other, their faded abstract aesthetic suddenly silhouetting against the horizon. The bus moved through a chiaroscuro of green valleys and rocky cliffsides: along narrow riverbeds full of cold, stony echoes, or dangerous precipices staring down hundreds of feet into fields of maize or millet with solitary cottages dotting the stepped hillside, half in shade, and half reflecting a curious golden light. But at the very next turn the view vanished and, without a warning, the flank of the mountain swallowed us. Inside, the air tasted metallic, and sounds were harsher on the ear. For a long while we moved in a tight wet darkness as if through a vein in the rock. Unpleasantness rose in my throat; I began to slowly suffocate. Then in the distance a spot of light filtered in, grew in size, took hold of me at last. It was like this, on the very edge of consciousness, that I recall entering the vale of Kashmir.

Sometime later, the bus dropped the three of us on a market square off the main road to Srinagar. My uncle, wearing his hair long and sporting a beard, was waiting by the side of a caleche. Any number of them stood in a queue not far from the stop. The horses and the two-wheeled carriages had the look of a different century. My uncle, still in his sandals and shirtsleeves, not bothered at all by the developing chill, was of the same set. In the late afternoon, as we moved past them, the empty shops gave out flickering patterns of color from their dim interiors, and the slanting red and green roofs of the square were very beautiful against the falling sky. Here and there newborn clouds rose suddenly from the midst of cedars and dissolved with a pink flush on the rocky rise. The entire scene was reminiscent of my book of German fairy tales back home, with animals and cottages popping out at you from a background of thickly forested cardboard pages. That grandeur, the romance of the mountains, in truth merely an enchantment with the ideal—with nature's majestic forms pulling you back into myth—had come to me early. When with the passage of years this private happiness couldn't be realized or awakened for long durations, it left a terrible lack that might have been my undoing had not literature come and steadied me, showing the path, ill-lit though it was often, that cut straight through the forest of the world.

How distilled the facts of that trip are in my mind; it is as if the years and decades had worked in reverse to sharpen the impressions: those last slow miles to the village, the narrow bridge over the river, and the reddening vast above the green velvety landscape across which the passive horse pulled the caleche with an old, practised instinct. Although I was barely four then, it seems to me today, nearly two score years later, that with only a slight extra effort I could count the grains of dust that hung on the leaves by the side of the path. I hear again my uncle telling me the names of things and places; I turn back to look at my father in his light tweed jacket, his hair black as a raven's wing and his mustache neatly trimmed, the delight of homecoming like a smell emanating from his person. And my mother(?), the city girl with the shawl tight round her shoulders, suspended between fatigue and anxiety as she gazes solemnly into the molecules of air vanishing in the wake of our passage.

They look young in my memory, far younger than I am now, all the denizens of that village, even the ones who in truth were quite old. Like people with a sudden presentiment of their death, I see events from my childhood with a startling clarity, while yesterday and the day before have the grainy, fogged out feel of old film. Partly because it was our last such trip together; partly because the month was the harbinger of upheavals to come; but perhaps also because nearly five years after my father's passing, anything touching his life quickly comes into focus, a belated grieving of sorts, the almost daily nightmares that would wake me in the dark of the cottage have, after so long a time, made their surprising return. Scarcely have I fallen asleep than the walls of my room are made of lath again. I can feel the plaster and smell the limewash in the air. The dread of those walls inching ever closer is very real in my sleep, so when they suddenly catch fire and are about to crush me, I wake up with the taste of ash in my mouth and the whole of that period, the entire vista down to the last minute detail, rises untarnished, like Proust's Combray, before my smarting eyes. My parents lift me up and rush outside. And away from the circle of homes, near the stand of aspens at the foot of the hill round which the river bends out of view, my cough finally eases. Looking down from my perch, I can make out the number twelve in the tiny blue square of my father's Japanese watch. My mother speaks to him in hushed tones and in the ink-flow of the night the constellations dip lower, gently listening in. Their gleam is at our feet as we wait in that mountainous solitude, the three visitors from the plains, before I am calm enough to return indoors.

What had I heard that I'd so taken to heart without knowing? Something about the fire that had pushed my grandfather's family to the edge of ruin? A careless line, dropped in my presence, regarding the disturbing incidents that were beginning to occur with a certain periodicity? Or was it simply my child's intuition offering a peek into the future, the burning of the cottage and the adjoining family home—a fiery glimpse into the destiny of that land and its culture, into the killings and exodus to come less than six years hence? Madness of a kind, a violent fanaticism fed and encouraged from across the border, slowly simmered beneath the unearthly beauty of the place, beneath the daily rounds of the muezzin's plaintive call to the faithful.

But for now, this beauty was enough. It filled the heart and drowned the senses. Every little town boasted a spring or a lake you had to visit. One went up and down in bus or gig past fields of paddy and sometimes saffron. One crossed orchards of apple and apricot; flowerbeds, willows and maples, almond and walnut trees, filled your vision. Entire hills watered by thin icy channels were thick with cedars that grew quite close together; their boles, chasing the light, rose a hundred feet and more into the sky. Near the treeline, slow-moving ice from the jagged peaks above spread its glacial fingers through the green fuzz, while here and there moraines flared in the noon sun like arteries carrying the forest's lifeblood. The eye could not bear the weight of this scene for long. It descended to earth quickly and, finding its measure, was relieved to follow the slope that fell away from the road where white dots quivered and were suddenly sheep.

In Srinagar, the market squares were messier; men in *pherans*, idle already by two o'clock, smoked hookahs beside dark doorways, thin figures of repose amid the rising din of the street. Under the eaves and rotting corbels, around the peeling shutters of the small top floor windows where a pale face could sometimes be glimpsed, soot had slowly collected and hardened. It projected an almost medieval effect over the tight façades, the feel of a harsh unfinished charcoal sketch. But beyond the narrow lanes of the old town, past the running gutters and butcher shops, the view magically lifted, and the extreme contrast was instantly lessened. Now the colorful shaded gondolas on the Dal, the thousand bells from the temple on the hill crashing into islands of cloud and pouring down on land and water, the flower gardens and fountains at the northern end of the lake, the wavy ranges catching the softening sun on their bleached pinnacles were all part of a never-ending spell cast by some benefic deity. From the somberness of a sketch to the lightness of a watercolor it seemed only the shortest of walks.

The emotion born of that pastoral spectacle has remained with me, having traversed a great distance without the least loss of energy. How well these words of Gracq fit my feelings! Even today, for instance, I can recall the hushed coming of autumn to that virescent landscape. At first, lone spots of red and yellow amid the green scenery. Then, slowly, tonal streaks enlarging into irregular patches like blood through a piece of gauze— until one morning, unexpectedly, the entire hillside stitched together in a vivid tapestry of delight. How had it happened, this chromatic miracle, under my ever-careful daily watch? The low skies and gray light, the dewy silence that hung well into the afternoon, muted the flashing saffroned leaves of the chinar, submerged the many shades of the Himalayan flora, so that the effect was subtle and holistic, striking deep into the soul, utterly inexplicable. When light was stronger, the scale was reduced; hues became saturated and required pointed attention. Things were again of this earth, somehow less memorable. One moved slowly from tree to tree to absorb all that glitter, and the other world, the one greater than the sum of its parts, faded unnoticed back into the rocky terrain.

Soft, beautifully chromatic days and sleep-deprived, terror-filled nights. I was too little to understand or speak out, but the feeling of skirting some great unraveling had been growing within me. And just as autumn was peaking in the valley, terror swiftly breached the banks of the dark and rushed headlong into our lives. News was relayed on the radio of Prime Minister Gandhi's assassination in Delhi by her own Sikh bodyguards. Riots broke out soon after and curfew was imposed in many parts of north India. On the highway through the mountains by which we had come, civilian traffic was abruptly halted, and Kashmir, just like that, was cut off from the rest of the country. Over the next several days, as winter began its steady descent from the high passes of the Karakoram, when all that erstwhile color flowing through the trees pooled at the foot of the bare, brush like forest, when a thick mist rose from the lakes and fields of the darkening vale that made lanterns necessary at three in the afternoon, a queer silence—a growing trepidation—hung heavy over the famed Himalayan paradise.

South of the mountains, in the plains of Punjab, through fields that had appeared so tranquil from the passing train, secessionist sentiment had been spreading for some time. It now gained a fever pitch; and men, trained and armed and facilitated next door, began to cross the border in large numbers. Internal strife grew and the social fabric of the region came under tremendous strain. Old scars of partition still showed across the body politic, and with the sudden rise in violence, painful memories of that time were quickly revived. The state, wary of looking weak and fearing further fragmentation of its territories, acted with a rare resolve. By the time winter was over, a long cycle of terror and alienation had commenced.

But for the strategists of the military junta in Pakistan, the insurgency in Punjab was merely a test run for Kashmir. Its success, the ease with which it spread across the entire state checkmating the policymakers in New Delhi, encouraged them to act with a rash boldness they didn't think they possessed after successive defeats in war. The long and treacherous border, carved artificially by a withdrawing colonial power with scant regard for the history of the place, was made yet more porous by sympathizers on either side. In the mountains, where the extreme terrain presented serious surveillance difficulties, it was the easier to infiltrate.

For a while, Punjab burned and Kashmir stayed cool. Then tongues of flame leapt higher to lick the mountains and Kashmir began to kindle. Years later, when calm once more reigned over the fields of Punjab, countless streams of lava still flowed through the land of the lotus bloom.

Of course, the Eighties were also the final years of the Cold War: frosty over the Atlantic; searing hot across Asia. The revolution in Iran, the hostilities in the Persian Gulf, the ever worsening Soviet-Afghan conflict had by turns destabilized the entire Middle East and transformed India's neighborhood into a geopolitical minefield where armed, radicalized guerrillas, incentivised by the West, terrorised their own people as they fought the enemy power to the north. The junta, clear-sighted, never one to pass up the opportunity for quick profits, was only too willing to oblige distant foreigners in their proxy wars around the region. Its officers, working at the behest of the Americans, got rich training and arming the mujahideen fighting the Russians in the dusty countryside. And since the camps were already functional, the supply of money generous, the propaganda handy, did it not stand to reason to drill a few extra men and send them eastward? Needling India, Soviet Russia's closest ally, keeping it embroiled in internal conflicts, was merely the surplus reward of a well thought out strategy. From China to Arabia interests seemed to have swiftly aligned, opening a chasm across which one old ally could not come to the aid of another. On the chessboard of history and realpolitik, India suddenly looked weak and cornered, ready to reap a bitter harvest for the past romantic attitudes of its leaders.

Picnics and peace marches in Europe, rampant bigotry and daylight murders in Kashmir. As the Union of the Soviet Socialist Republics was coming apart at the seams, extremist indoctrination was on the rise in the valley. By the time the Berlin Wall fell, rule of law, the state's monopoly on violence, had totally collapsed in most towns and villages.

'Things are fast slipping out of control,' a friend of my father called to warn him. 'The mosques spew venom daily, and their invective, imported from abroad, is making people edgy. The sentiment has completely soured. Delhi must act quickly else I fear the damage won't be reversible.' He had availed himself of the preacher's sharp inflammatory monologue during the Friday prayers. Afterward he had gone straight to the village to impress upon my grandparents the urgency to move away for a few months. 'Until things improve a little,' he said to comfort them. But my grandparents had known no other way of life and were unwilling to leave.

'When this boils over,' the friend didn't mince his words, 'the police will simply stand aside and watch the slaughter. The politicians here are almost wishing for it. They know exactly which side their bread is buttered.

It might happen tomorrow. It may not happen for six months. Either way, they are not safe here anymore. You simply must reason with them.'

So five years after that fateful autumn in Kashmir, I found my grandparents one morning at our home in Delhi. I was nine at the time and my sister, born a year after our return from the valley, was of the same age as I had been then. Knowing only one set of grandparents, she was now granted the opportunity to learn about another. She was both intrigued and confused by their presence. I, on the other hand, to my later regret, was cool toward them. In my mind, they belonged to that fairy tale world of my childhood, and their unexpected appearance in our house, far away from the lure of the mountains, the air of loss and abstraction doggedly clinging to them, diminished their stature and made me stay away. I knew something strange had happened, but whenever I tried to ask my mother, she would give me the look which said: 'Why, what a silly question! Now run along and let me work.' It was in my sister that my grandmother found solace over the ensuing weeks and months, and it was through her, too, that she eventually reconciled to this new life in the city, even as my grandfather grew more and more solitary with each passing day, poring over the news for hours on end to make sense of the alarming developments that were taking place in Kashmir.

When later my father had found suitable accommodations for them, my sister would often accompany him to their place on weekends. Her arrival never failed to cheer up my grandmother, and every now and then, in the short time still left her, it was possible to witness afresh a hint of the same affection and tenderness she had bestowed on me so freely in an earlier, happier time.

It was a while before my parents could make a trip back to the village, a trip not without its risks, for the area had continued to report significant militant activity right into the present. Just days before their visit, armed men had attacked a passing military convoy in the very square where once you would have emerged from the bus and hopped onto a waiting gig to be driven across the green tranquil landscape under summer's fading light. They spent hardly any time in the village. My father, to my mother's great annoyance, ignored her earlier advice to behave like tourists that didn't speak the language. After their return to Srinagar the same evening, my father said to me on the phone that the place was near unrecognizable, and that the ruins of the old family home still stood by the stream. By then, my grandmother had been dead for many years and my grandfather, who

I barely saw now, lived a withdrawn, out-of-the-way life with one of my uncles in another part of the city.

'Won't you take me there, captain?' Herman would say to me in the days we were still living and working in Delhi. But up until the moment I found myself on the short flight to Srinagar, I hadn't really given the notion much thought. Often had we yielded to the pull of the mountains, moving through them like swallows above a field at dusk, lately even climbing the rim of the earth with Rosamund by our side, a trip so unexpected and life-altering it had taken an unknown foreigner and turned her into a bosom friend, and yet, we had always avoided Kashmir.

It was for good reason. There were the cherished memories of the past I did not wish to disturb, memories overlaid with the pain of others I had shared unknowingly, vicariously, while growing up. It seemed unnecessary to invoke and cancel them in the harsh light of day. And in this I was not wrong. For I soon found what I was expecting to find. A kind of brokered peace had returned to the valley, but Srinagar still resembled a city under siege: sandbagged checkpoints; rolls of barbed wire cordoning off street sections; sudden diversions placed before slogan-sprawled shopfronts, abandoned, bullet-holed walls, battle fatigues zooming in and out of view at certain corners.

The delicate syncretic culture of the valley—a result of the slow, agonizing sublimation of centuries of suffering under foreign rule—was long dead. But the dream of an Islamic caliphate, cunningly cultivated among half the citizenry, had alas not come to fruition. Instead, twenty years of violence and stasis had left the people grossly alienated who lived confused half-lives in the midst of a burgeoning war economy. Equal parts nervy and hostile, they were used to being pampered and exploited by disparate groups forever working the countless levers of power in the state.

Srinagar: The City of Shri, consort of Vishnu and the splendor of the universe. Where had the splendor vanished? The town which in my childhood had been merely old and rustic, was now pitifully ugly and run down. What accentuated its ramshackle air was the presence of homes and streets that spoke of riches ill-gotten. Money had poured into the valley from every side, yet it had not moved freely: except the occasional shiny new bungalow highlighting the sordidness around, there was little to show for it. Money had come and money had congealed like a clot on the skin of the town. It had benefited only a few. Next to the derelict cottage, the nicely trimmed yews of the politician's property. The deep rot, the complete moral and imaginative failure of those involved, was apparent in a glance. And as if to lend credence to this instinct, to add insult to injury, the sight of the Jhelum from the choked and dirty lanes of the bazaar was one of stagnation and filth. The river, of which there were hymns in the *Rig Veda*, was the very same Hydaspes the Greek army had crossed in flood to enter India two millennia ago. It now creamed along the embankment in florescent scum. On the footbridge from where we looked, a bearded man came and stood beside us and spat affectedly into the water.

'What a mess!' sighed Herman. 'Let's head out while there's still light.' He had little desire to see the sights and wanted to get up into the mountains before nightfall. Next morning though, his mood had clearly lifted. He hurriedly drove me out of bed to point at the luminous south face of Nanga Parbat wreathed in mist and floating above the chain of peaks to the north. While I watched a lammergeier ride the thermal against this dramatic glacial background, Herman spoke with my father on the phone and took mental notes. We ended up staying a fortnight in that solitary glade where every day shepherds passed by our cottage guiding their flocks to lower ground. We walked a part of the way with them, the murmur of sheep at our elbow, returning, as evening fell, by a steep forest path where we had been warned bears were often sighted. 'Seldom,' said Herman, 'have I felt so light and free. Could it be we died at the previous bend and are now in heaven?'

'Better not get too comfortable. Any minute here a stray bullet can kill you. Paradise, if there's one, comes much later.'

'Look, there: moonrise!'

Into the valley far away, nestled between the shoulders of lesser hills, night had arrived already, and lights were twinkling dimly through a film of woodsmoke from the kitchen fires below. At eye level, across the empty darkened landscape, the silver snowfields blanketing the jagged slate pinnacles were magical to behold against the advancing shadows.

So much pain, so much corruption, I could sense my friend thinking, cradled by such sublimity and grandeur. Amid the earth's bounty, this shriveled crop of man's endless folly.

For all the years my father had been unable or unwilling to go back, his love for the mountains had nonetheless remained strong, even deepened. Time and again he was pulled toward those remote vistas by some unknown force that both attracted and disturbed him. In their protection, I believe, he slipped free of his cares, the press of the past and the burdens of the present. Perhaps there he was given the vision of another life, one that might have been possible under different circumstances, a life wholly immersed in nature like in the books of his youth: solitary, blissful, easy, and wild. A private Shangri-La where time ceased and pain had no purchase. The peaks rose sheer and changeless around him, and his spirit, keeping pace, following its own stepped echo, rose steadily with them.

I recall how in my childhood he often went trekking to the base of remote glaciers in the Himalayas, or to look from up close but not climb the shinning summits of Nanda Devi, Kanchenjunga, and Everest. Each year in spring or autumn he would be gone for two or three weeks, and I would think of him from the comfort of my mother's former home, a tiny dark figure far off at the foot of this or that eight-thousander. Upon his return, the rubber soles of his hiking boots still carried the mud from those elevations, and when no one was looking I would carefully scrape it off into one palm and take a pinch and rub between my fingers.

Before my sister was born and for a while thereafter, the memory of my parents was a memory of vague presences. Easily the happiest period of my life, it was spent mostly in the bosom of my mother's family. The love of my grandparents and my young unmarried aunts—what patient, benevolent beings!—filled my entire horizon. I can still summon up at will my grandfather's flat with the mulberry tree in the back garden beneath whose low shade I would rush after play to find my grandmother relaxing on a string cot. I liked rubbing my nose into her muslin cheeks and making her laugh, and she, on her part, would pluck the tiny hanging fruit from the nearest branch and promptly transfer it to my mouth. The bedroom windows upstairs neatly framed the giant figs in the park that always looked so menacing on stormy nights, but whose otherwise rustic charm was pleasing to catch in the morning sun. A strip of fallow ground and several rows of poplars separated the narrow-gauge railway from the colony of flats on one side, and late at night as if from some previous life the sound of the goods train whistling past would gently enter and exit my sleep. 'I too am seized,' Heine had written, 'by the mysterious thrill of the distant sound!' With what difficulty I'd suppressed the shiver the poet's words had given me when I first chanced upon them years later in a small shop with narrow, sunken shelves falling into disrepair.

Into this veritable haven then, a fantasy world born of a child's trust and repose, my father would descend like a spirit of the mountains and sweep me up in his strong arms. The citrusy coolness of pine and juniper bush still clung to his frame, while behind him, in the direction from which he had just arrived, the wind could be seen splicing cirrus clouds through the blue dome of the sky.

Two decades hence, it was the memory of this very period, triggered by the sight of those sprawling trees shading the promenade on Balmoral Beach in Sydney, that had brought on the sadness which had signaled to me the end of my freedom, but also—surprisingly—the end of my youth. In a matter of moments and for no apparent reason, I seemed to have crossed prematurely into middle age. And over the following weeks and months, my attitudes, too, suffered a great change, became the attitudes of a much older person. Scarcely four years earlier, uncertain about the future course of my life, I had taken those walks along the canal lined with narrowboats on the other side of the world. But now that things had turned out not unfavorably, now that I had been given a second chance to make a clean start, to lunge at the literary life with both hands, now that my pursuits were aligned with my larger aims, so to speak, I seemed to balk at even the simplest of joys to Rita's great consternation. While neither of us was the person from before the time of the crash, she had traveled to Australia with the intent of reviving that happy past, of at last having with me the kind of life that never could have been possible in England. My seemingly easy task was to merely indulge her a little, to quietly keep watch as she petitioned fate to help parlay her meager gains into big winnings. But the change that had come in me in the intervening years was too hard to conceal; and although we were considerate toward each other, we were seldom on the same page. There was pain between us, a kind of blunted hurt that we both tried to ignore, but which erupted every now and then like a rash of the skin. When it subsided, it left behind a cool languor that lasted for weeks on end—a state that rather than breaking things up completely, worked only to tighten our marriage and our sorrow.

Later, in the midst of the great emptiness that had come to fill my life, this early phase of our marriage seemed to me to be burdened with needless pride and impatience, bathed in the diffused afterglow of melancholy that had we been a little more careful might have healed our dispirited hearts and preserved our strengths and passions for the future.

On the mornings I drove him to what would prove to be his last few chemo sessions, the wall of silence encasing my father seemed well-nigh impregnable. He sat very still by my side as we moved through the January fogs, gently shaking his head each time in response to my feeble attempts at conversation. A hint of warmth radiated from his eyes at such moments, perhaps even a bit of regret for putting us all through what by then he felt to be the sheer inconvenience of dying slowly. Far away from the bridge where the air was beginning to clear, a pair of barges rested on the blackish water, and towering over the weedy banks rose in straight lines the silent chimneys of the power station, their tops lost in the winter pall that hung quite low at this time of the year.

Fathers and Sons. Fraying bonds in the wintry tide. The dawn mists low over the river, hanging tentative like a half-visited dread.

Half attempts at small talk. Half-hearted, barely enough to mask the unease. The gulf that lay between us in those fluid moments was increasingly difficult to cross. I knew how much it cost him to speak; how much he disliked using his hands to block the newly opened stoma in the neck so that the device installed inside might produce sound vaguely resembling a voice. Yet I feared more his total lapse into silence and the desire, quite strong now, to remain permanently in the void. At this late stage of his life, knowing full well his nature and the reserves of courage still at his disposal, I felt I could hardly leave anything to chance.

A blast of horns through the gray air, their notes pressing firm against the chest. Dim golden echoes beneath heavy, nebulous words too late to voice.

Like bassoons tuning up before a performance, the city noise came ricocheting back in a lower key, soft if resonant, through a cloud of words unformed and unspoken.

An entire year had passed since my father's long and difficult laryngectomy, which instead of easing his physical and mental suffering had in fact gradually worsened it. Over eleven arduous hours in the operating room, his neck and a part of his head had been completely hollowed out. And now what the doctors had feared all along had come to pass. To inject yet more cytotoxic drugs through an already broken body seemed to be their only remedy for the worsening metastasis of the lungs.

Even with the disease ravaging unbeknown through him over several months preceding the surgery, even with his voice fading to a hoarse whisper as the strange malignancy gripped and crushed his larynx, my father had appeared in better form than at any time after the operation. On the day he was scheduled to be admitted to the hospital, he had even expressed the wish to go for a walk. He didn't seem to feel much pain, or he didn't show it. Very probably, had we not rushed him into surgery, the cancer would have spread to his brain before long, and he would have quietly slipped into coma and passed away in his sleep. It was paradoxically our desperate attempt to prolong his life that was the cause of all his subsequent physical and mental anguish, and that had bit by bit destroyed his body and his soul.

I had never once seen my father ill. Not even a head cold or a fever. Other than his trips into the mountains, which ceased completely during the latter part of my adolescence, he had never taken a day's leave from work. To see him this ill then, to keep him company as he was slowly fading away, was both new and unfathomable to me. Driving through the morning traffic, I would steal glances at him, and find him looking straight ahead with an abstracted air, disappeared into himself, rubbing his fingers together under his nose, the gestures of a man befuddled by the grand unfolding, the stark inevitability of fate, but somehow still in control of himself. It came to me that they were gestures right out of an early poem by Michael Hofmann. *The invited audience applauds on cue—those steady couples in their late twenties, well-dressed and supplied with contraceptives.* . . How cruel to begin this way a poem on death, with fulfilment running deep and nary a thought of the future. The image behind those words remembered on the spur of the moment, the fierce juxtaposition born of the poet's genius but perhaps also his love and his fear, was like poison to me. Youthful passions beneath the peel of bourgeois respectability, bodies provisionally sated enjoying sentimental music in the reddened dark of the poem's atmosphere, while here, across the gearbox, barely a foot away, the skeletal thighs in the woolen pants feeling the light but unmistakable press of death's hand.

All day in the hospital while my father received his treatment, my thoughts kept returning to Rita, patient and lonely on the other side of the world. That time we had gone to hear Puccini for our anniversary, trying to forget the gray present in the dazzling chromatic display of the set. *La Bohème* in a new time and a new setting, announced the brochure. Not Paris of the nineteenth century, but Berlin in the final months of the Weimar era. What did it matter to us, desperate souls looking for a little distraction? We could never have been one of Hofmann's happy couples, enjoying Mantovani's sentimental melodies from the plush safety of our ignorance. We kept up the appearances through the evening, but no warmth reached us from the stage. We were like tourists stranded in a foreign country after the initial rush of excitement has worn off, lacking the correct semiotic codes and superficially taking in the sights, a little bored, a little underwhelmed. The burlesque club, the costumes and the mores suggested to me as much Montmartre as Berlin, but the gaiety, the edgy euphoria of the players showed a society on the verge of collapse. Once I thought I even detected in Marcello's baritone the ominous rumblings of history. Outside, the wind in the harbor had turned chilly, and Rita took my arm the moment we emerged from the shells of the famous building, staying close and not speaking until we had reached the station at Circular Quay.

'The house has such charm,' Rita had remarked in the early days of our move to America. 'The house has. . .'

'Cosmicity,' I offered, trying not to sound too grand.

She seemed to consider this. 'Yes, that,' she said and got into bed. A bird sang in the cottonwood outside the window. I came into the living room and went out on the balcony.

How I wish I could reclaim those summer evenings helping you take the measure of yourself on a new continent! To feel once more the delightful purity of first impressions. After seven years of living under southern skies, I had again come north. Right into the heart of the country, the thought never left me as I watched the seasons change that first year. The geology here was old and intricate, stretching back to the Triassic, lending its maturity to shapes and patterns one observed overground. Nary an edge or a sharp angle anywhere; no sudden, sweeping elevations to trouble the mind. Just rolling hills and fields and coppices watered by countless clear streams hurrying away to the Hudson. Not very different it looked from the interior of England where we had been traveling barely a month ago. And yet, at least in the beginning, the place fed my fantasy in quite another way. At certain moments, the mood would take hold of me, and I would imagine myself much further up the mainland, somewhere along the coast of Labrador Sea, for instance, gazing across the blue eternity and yearning for the Arctic tundra.

It came to me some months later, the reason for this recurring reverie. The stasis I had so unexpectedly walked into, this promise of a second, simpler life after long periods of uncertainty, had brought to the fore old, forgotten instincts that could make even the most ordinary of spaces shine with the golden light of the past. And to allow for this dizzying collapse of time, it was perhaps necessary to conjure up vast, changeless horizons stretching to the very ends of earth.

The soul held in abeyance and lost time regained. One felt a curious presence flow out from the tiniest of things; enter the flesh of the world; make the whole pulsate with some higher, hidden meaning.

Often in those first days, as the night deepened, there was hardly any breeze, or just about enough to make the silver show in the serrated birch leaves beyond the railing. The moon, larger each day, already more generous with itself than it had seemed to me on my recent Manhattan walks, would leave the clouds behind and, like a tilted flagon, pour its heady cascade into milky concavities suspended beneath marbled cliffs. It spilled out into the dark, this light, stippling the shadows and vanishing into the trees. But it could not reach me. By the time I went to bed, the silence was so complete that I could hear the creek half a mile away in the murmur of Rita's sleep.

And so, little by little, we eased into a kind of pastoral where we were more observers than participants. The earth offered its delights easily and asked from us nothing in return. The land simplified everything, held the affairs of the world at bay. It soaked up time and our sadness; made us patient and attentive. The elements played low over it and appeared to bend and magnify above our bruised, weakened selves.

Unexpected and memorable, this second home, this second childhood in the valley, and soon we were both grateful for it. As I got busy preparing for the new term, I couldn't help but notice the change that had come over Rita. A serenity had taken hold of her, had begun to chip away at the debris of years. She lay in the sun for hours, listening to the birds in the birch trees that fringed the balcony. She made the rounds of all the farm shops in the area, took up gardening, told me she wasn't going back to work ever. It was a joy to see her like this, free and easy, like she was sixteen again.

A love of books, like the love of mountains, had come to me from my father. And because he hadn't tried to instil this love in any way, it had come with the unmistakable force of destiny. Unfolding slowly, almost imperceptibly, it bestowed gifts and abilities that seemed to be not of this world. In my youth, I was constantly puzzled and surprised by this sudden enhancement of perception, by how far I could see into the backward drift of language, by what words were doing to me and what in turn I could do with them.

Literature had given me everything and later taken everything away.

It had left me with few alternatives, bit by bit made me useless for the real world. I had been swimming against the current for so long, sustained only by the intensity of my efforts, that once I had burnt through this intensity to the other side, there was hardly anything left to do.

But then the Fates, like in Virgil, had found their way. A piece or two moved by some invisible hand and the pawn suddenly found itself in the furthest rank, in a new role and with new powers.

Like a glacier releasing water very slowly, the hope of the literary life had come back to me, had given me enough to hold together and to keep moving. So on the first day of classes, the irony was not entirely lost on me that I had to instil in a room full of kids a belief in the power of words, which, until recently, I myself had been on the point of losing.

The start of the term kept me busy. New setting, new faces. I worked late into the nights before my lectures, said much in the classes, lost my audience halfway. 'Take it easy,' was the first thing Rosamund told me at the end of my second week. She had just returned to Providence after a month on the West Coast. 'Don't do their work for them,' she spoke in a quick even tone as if trying to get the mundane stuff out of the way. 'Begin by asking leading questions. Like they do in a trial. Remember your training from the old days,' she laughed into the phone.

Sweet Ariadne lightening the mood, offering me again a thread out of the labyrinth. The passage of years had not changed that. I held on to her words, that soothing stream of a voice filling the warm, periwinkle evenings to the brim.

Rosamund's work trip had coincided with my arrival in America. At first, she'd thought of delaying her departure by a few days, of seeing me in New York before flying out. 'It's been almost a decade!' she protested. But I persuaded her to not alter her plans. Of course, a part of me wanted to see her right away, yet a part of me had also hesitated, needed more time to unwind the effect of the years, perhaps even to ready myself for the certainty of finding her much changed—the death of the last remaining illusion of my youth.

We now made plans to meet. And at the end of September, I took the morning train to New York, running the reel in reverse, moving backward in time.

I went downstream with the river, past the lush hills under a brightening sky. Two months became two years, became ten. Herman's words rushed back to me in the quiet of the rail car. I, too, now saw what he had seen then: Rosamund amid rocks and wildflowers. But in my state of relative ease, I saw further, I heard more. I watched brown crags, fresh snow in their crevices, tear into passing clouds, ancient monasteries clutching their summits, about to slip any moment into the abyss. I felt the rush of the rivers flowing into one another. The dim tinkling of a thousand bells reached me across the ocher haze. And amid this cool dry eternity cradled by the Himalaya, just a little ahead of us, again was Rosamund.

I changed trains at Grand Central and came out at Union Square. It was as if I had walked into a different city from the one I had departed two months earlier. Not a cloud at that hour throwing a moving shadow across the tall structures. The light pierced through the ravines on every side. But it was only half past eleven, and the drama often heightened in the afternoon.

I began to walk toward Chelsea, to the address Rosamund had given me. Then I turned a corner and there she was, right in the line of my vision, looking even younger from when I had last seen her. It was the hair, now shorter, straighter, cleanly parted, ending just above the shoulder blades, that made prominent her lean figure, rolling back the years.

The light on the sidewalk was still soft. She stood at the very edge of it, close to some red flowers, the shadows deepening behind her. That pale blue shirt, hanging loose on her frame, made from the finest of materials, wasn't it the same one from so many summers ago? I saw the rouge on her lips and thought: 'Not all my illusions will die today.'

Her eyes absorbed my surprise completely as she came forward to welcome me. In her embrace, there was only honest emotion, a keen remembrance of our time together. The push of old glaciers far away in the hammock of the peaks defining the course of the swift, hooked river at our feet. It was as if we had come down from the mountains just yesterday.

Proust had written of the eyes of the Duchesse being of a color that resembled the sky above the forests of Guermantes. But it wasn't in Rosamund's cool, if lucid, gaze that I felt the old vistas rise to the surface again. Rather it was in the strangeness of first contact, the pressure of her fingers on my back, her cheek against my cheek, her smell, spreading easily through the recesses of memory, reminding me of the nights we'd slept huddled close in that unheated, drafty room at the foot of the cliff where the locals said the snow leopards came to shed their shyness in winter; in short, it was her immediate radiating presence on that sidewalk which gave back to me the sun and the wind and the sound of the mountain. Not in her eyes then (for I was closer to Rosamund in that moment than Marcel, swooning over Oriane in his youthful fancies, ever had any right to be), but in the very arc of her being did I see those skies, so high and clear at noon, suddenly shift and move, grow dark at the onset of evening, become a vast, invisible sieve that filtered in the light of faraway worlds.

She touched the hair above my temple and spoke in a tone I hadn't heard before: 'Still searching, Gir? Still looking? Whatever for?' And she hugged me again. 'But you're here now,' she added sotto voce.

Our first stop was a photography exhibition she'd wanted to see. I didn't care where we went as long as she went with me. She carried inside her, in every cell of her body, a cherished fragment of my past, complete and preserved from the ravages of time—a reminder of days so full of camaraderie and ardor that had we as much as raised our arms, we would have scratched the very knees of the gods.

On the way to the gallery, she told me she had spoken to Herman the previous night: 'We should head back to the hills,' she declared. 'It's been too long. We've been careless with ourselves. The years have slipped by. It's beginning to show.'

'On you?' I thought. 'Not in the least.'

'Is this what he suggested?' I said merely to keep the conversation going. I hadn't been this happy in years. It was a muted type of happiness that rather than rise to the surface did its work quietly.

'Yes. Although he seemed distracted at first.'

'Clearly, he misses you.'

'And you,' she responded with cheery readiness. 'Have you kept in touch with him? The writer, I mean. How ever did we find him in that inhospitable place?'

I told her that we still corresponded occasionally, and that, like her, I hadn't expected to find him. It was pure chance. I had merely been following a certain sentiment gleaned from a single book and an old interview, a thought traced through his words and raised to an extreme possibility over the course of months. The grainy monochrome photo on the back cover had done its bit to help, but the picture was two decades old, and, on that day, Kalan could have been anywhere except the one spot where I had found him: outside that dusty shed in the bazaar, waiting to collect the equipment that had been sent for him from a town on the other side of the mountains.

'He must be getting old now,' she mused. 'Past seventy, possibly older.

We should go soon,' she repeated in a firmer voice.

In the group being exhibited at the gallery, there was a set of photographs from an ongoing series that the artist had titled *Made in the Shade*. Self-portraits in carefully staged modern settings. Formally dressed figures, each a different projection of the artist, with lush, gorgeous curls or perfectly styled heads looking away from the camera. Soothing brown, yellow, and green tones from the fifties with hints of reds and evening blues in the furniture and the windows, respectively, taking you back to the days of film. There was much to admire here. These were really novel environmental portraits, moving, cleverly executed. In one of them, a woman—the artist—sat in a shaft of light engrossed in the pages of a magazine. The sun gleamed through her golden curls that fell like a curtain over the side of her face concealing it from view. The soft pastel tones of the model's pants and cardigan beautifully accented the mid-century scheme of the room, the self-effacing glow of the lamp outside the reach of the sun, and the broadleaved plant in the open window. The solitude of the photograph took me in, mysterious and enchanting like a painting from an earlier era. There was something of Hopper in it, although the vibe now was naturally upbeat, of an America that had positively jettisoned the Depression era gloominess. Its relaxed and confident mood stayed with me when later we sauntered to a café in West Village and talked straight into the evening.

We had much to say to each other and we said all we had to say. A silence fell between us like the silence of clouds moving in from the sea at that hour, flowing and luminous. Slowly, the sound of our own voices came back to us, layered now in the echoes of the past. For the first time that day, I began to notice things that were different about her, all the little ways, not immediately observable, in which she had most assuredly changed. The way love changes you. I kept listening. I kept responding. The sounds of the street passed through us, and the city sank into a lucid abstraction just at the edge of meaning.

On the train taking me home, I wondered whether I hadn't dreamt up the whole thing, whether in fact Rosamund was nothing but a figment of my own imagination. Her absence always left this peculiar impression as if she had appeared out of nowhere just the minute before. Our first meeting that summer in Delhi had been like this too.

Half a mile from the train station, on the cusp of the old and the new cities, near the arched railway bridge the approach to which got flooded each year in the rainy months, there was a bar called *Bliss Mountain*. It'd had a long and checkered history. It had begun as a cabaret patronized by the officers of the Raj during the Thirties, situated at the northern end of the new imperial city so recently risen from the rock bed of the Aravalis. Apocryphal surely, but even Kipling was rumored to have visited the place. In those days, it was said, news from the ends of the empire, from Burma to Afghanistan, from beyond the Pamirs, from places as far away as Samarkand and the Caucasus, hung in the air, and often going to dine there was a better way to get hold of the happenings than the evening newssheet.

After the war, once the British were gone, the nightclub, like so many relics of the era, had appeared out of place, even a little ridiculous, and nobody had known what to do with it. For a while, it had trudged along, then, with the previous management selling out, had slowly gone to seed. After a drug deal had been busted, gunshots exchanged, three dead, a woman among them, the police had sealed it off.

But the club was too close to the center of things to remain shackled to the courts forever. At some point, it was purchased in a distress sale, refurbished in new money, and opened to a mixed clientele never very far away. When, years later, I began to go there with a few friends, it was already in decline. The sharpness of its lines, like its earlier patrons, like the price of its martinis, had faded; the furniture had sagged, the paint on the walls had turned, and the fire in the stained-glass panes had cooled and become dull. Only bits of the past survived in a few paintings high up in the shadows, wreathed in the spider scrawl of time.

To come up the low flight of steps dodging the heat of the day through the frosted-glass door into the cool shade of the long room; to see feeble light turn in glass and ice, burnish wood and stone, enter dark matter; to hear the distant but familiar voices floating above a faint scent of danger— this was how the weekly ritual began. All that history, all that romance, the ever-moving cycles of time, laughter of friends, and yet, the place had needed Rosamund to complete the picture.

It was to Bliss Mountain that Gina or the fates had brought Rosamund.

Before the year was over Gina was gone, dead by her own hand, and Rosamund had returned to America. But a friendship forged over those two burning months had become something of an anchor for my mental and spiritual life. Rosamund was Gina's parting gift. They had met at a conference in Singapore and Gina had learnt of Rosamund's plan to travel to India, that in fact she was leaving the day after on the same flight as her.

Strange destinies fed by banal encounters.

We misread each other on that first meeting. It was still hot at five in the afternoon when I reached the bar. I had just come off the phone with Rita. We had been making each other miserable. Things were getting difficult in London. The crisis that had begun as a faint rumor in distant places had in no time grown into a giant wrecking ball, which, in quick succession, had crashed the grand citadels of finance in the West. There was pain on the streets and lay-offs in the glass towers higher up. Those, like Rita, who until recently had been able to fend off the more immediate effects of the downturn were now under more and more strain each day. It didn't help that by then I had cut myself loose from that world and was prepared to drift even further. So when I walked past the stained glass windows into the cool of the room, all I was looking for was the company of old friends in a familiar setting. I was not prepared to find among them a stranger of such unsettling beauty. My greeting perhaps was less than friendly, and Rosamund's impression of me couldn't have been ideal, certainly not what she might have expected after all that Gina had told her.

It wasn't until the evening after when we were able to form a proper opinion of one another. In the bar, I had seen Rosamund talk animatedly with Herman, and I'd thought of asking him later about her. But before I could do anything, the two were at my doorstep. I signaled for them to come up to the terrace. Herman was carrying a pack of beer, and I was glad Rosamund was with him.

'They've been firing people at the bank all week,' Herman said, lighting a cigarette. 'Shutting the very operation I help build last year. So now I must force everyone out.' For his many services, not least at this crucial hour, the bank had offered to relocate him to another department or office. But Herman was fed up. 'Last exit interviews left to do, then I'm going on a long leave. It might be that I never go back.'

Rosamund looked like she knew what Herman was saying. He was merely repeating for my benefit what he had already told her on the way to my flat. There was nothing peculiar in this. When Herman liked someone, he included them fully into his life. That was his nature. It was what made him instantly approachable in any gathering. Both men and women found his honesty thoroughly disarming and often did not hesitate to offer him their deepest confidences, sometimes almost against their will. He was good at what he did, had risen fast at the bank, but he didn't much care for this kind of thing. Therefore, he could talk candidly about a difficult day at work with someone he had just met. Books, certain nagging philosophical doubts, the inner meaning of things: these, on the other hand, were matters he was greatly circumspect about and rarely, if ever, discussed with others.

'I'm coming behind you,' he went on, 'or with you if you could be made to wait a little.'

I handed them each a beer and hinted that I must leave soon.

'You have a lead?' Herman was suddenly interested.

'A hunch. Not even maybe. I'll call and let you know where I am. This way I might save you some time while I figure out the best route.'

The three of us talked awhile and then went out to dinner. The pandemonium on the other side of the world had not yet reached us, or not to the extent that you couldn't dine in peace with friends. Rosamund said that Gina was taking her to see the salt marshes. 'We should be back by the end of the week,' she added.

'You know where that is?' Herman jumped in. 'The Rann, I mean.'

I looked at Rosamund's bright face, her discerning blue eyes, the slim yet strong arms. Was it the best time for this kind of excursion halfway across the desert? But then she was already getting used to the heat.

'How much worse can it get?' Herman finally conceded. 'Besides, once the sun goes down, it gets all nice and starry in a hurry. A great redness stretches beyond the luminous flats as if for the last time. You finally begin to understand what Rothko was after.'

Over the meal Herman brought Rosamund up to date on my proposed trip. She should have thought me crazy, going in search of someone about whom I knew almost nothing. But I could see she was curious, was watching me almost half-admiringly. The whole thing was a fantasy, born out of my impatience to go looking for the other life, to test myself a little at the edge of things. Kalan, in the beginning anyway, was simply the excuse I had needed.

Two weeks later we were in the mountains. The three of us—what an unlikely trio!—on those bare, high slopes worlds away from civilization! How had it come to pass?

Summer was finally over. Mornings and evenings were now noticeably cooler in the valley. One day leaving class my sight fell on a lone leaf whose edges were outlined in crimson as if an invisible sun was rising from its green depths. Before long the entire countryside was submerged in bounties of red and gold. For the very first time since my childhood, I was in the grip of a proper autumn, whose silent approach, just as that autumn so many years ago in Kashmir, had taken me completely by surprise. Color flashed far and wide, time telescoped, and a curious sensation entered and left the soul. Every second somewhere in the valley, a leaf came floating down in its own quantum of silence: a tiny chromatic event of indescribable beauty. The developing chill in the air was a half-remembered prophecy. I began to go out for walks regularly. Sometimes Rita accompanied me, but mostly I went alone.

For a while I moved alongside the motorway with cars zipping past on their way to New York. Then I went off the main road taking a trail through the trees that after a mile or so ended in a glade with the shape of distant hills first fading then darkening in the softening light. Once, returning from work, and after a brief spell of rain in the afternoon, I went out along the familiar route. Turning away from the busy road, I happened to brush past a low, spreading branch. A shiver went through me, but I didn't take any note of it. When I came out of the wood, I sat on a rock and watched clusters of mist and cloud push open the ray-fan of the declining sun and float down the knoll into the line of trees. The cloud remained inside the bush, and the color, sharp just some moments ago, was now barely visible.

Men remoter than mountains
Women invisible in music and motion and color.

These words of Wallace Stevens, impulsively remembered, were like a bridge across which a different, hidden self quietly left me and vanished into the setting.

I don't know how long I kept staring at that scene, but when at last I emerged from my reverie, I found that my collar was wet and that tears were still flowing down my face and on to my chest.

The term ended, but the idyll continued. Trees stood stark and erect in a bed of rotting leaves. Giant pylons, suddenly sad and dramatic amid all that bareness, stretched across the emptying landscape in a never-ending line. It was already our sixth month in the valley. The start of the new year would bring more cold—a kind of cold neither of us was ready for. A sharp, silent cold in which hidden, unresolved grief rises to the surface. I seemed to have aged more quickly in the past months, and now, free for the time being from my professional worries, I wished for nothing more than to sit still and take stock.

By and by winter deepened and with it my solitude. For long periods I leaned in the window watching the light recede and the sky turn, listening to the geese call in a long chaotic jumble from the neighboring field. Their loud, melancholy cackle stretched over the hard earth, loosening the circles of thought, and easing yet further my hesitant grip on the world. The eye traveled in a north-easterly direction over the gray tips of the wintry forest to the mauve-blue bulk of the hills, and every now and then I would catch myself thinking: at least, there's this.

My thoughts more and more were of the last days of my father, his unfailing forbearance, except toward the very end, in the face of approaching death. That time I sat by his side as the nurse probed his slack, wasted arm, puncturing the skin here and there to locate the right vein to push the drug in. Soon he had gone past all needling and pain. The dreadful cough had subsided; his breathing was light but even. For the last half hour, I had been distractedly thumbing through De Quincey's essay about the English Mail-Coach. *Seven atmospheres of sleep*, I now read, *seemed resting upon him*. I looked up from the page to glance at the supine figure of my father, the outstretched arm through which the chemicals were coursing, the dark visions behind the closed lids that would never come to light.

Driving to the hospital earlier that morning, taking a different bridge over the misted river, we had passed the exhibition grounds where in times past my father had taken me to the book fair each year. Little had remained in my mind of those visits, but the image of the stalls flooded with volumes from Russia was still fresh in me. Forbidding tomes printed on cheap paper with shiny covers in light pastels. They seemed to contain within them the whole of that depressing era, the sad, sluggish mood of the Eighties. Books written by men whose long, confusing names I could barely pronounce. Why then did my father love them so? I owed my first Chekhov, left unread for years afterward, to one such visit.

When I next strayed from the book, my father was awake and gazing right through me. He didn't know who or what he was looking at. Then slowly the pain returned and with it the memory. I asked him if he needed anything. He smiled faintly, shook his head, and closed his eyes. *The sea, the atmosphere, the light, bore an orchestral part in this universal lull. Moonlight, and the first timid tremblings of the dawn, were now blending; and the blendings were brought into a still more exquisite state of unity, by a slight silvery mist, motionless and dreamy, that covered the woods and fields, but with a veil of equable transparency.*

My left hand held his left ankle lightly. I didn't want to let go of him. But the hooves of death rushing at him with the terrifying speed of thirteen miles an hour could be heard clearly in the quiet of the room. *Glance of eye, thought of man, wing of angel, which of these had speed enough to sweep between the question and the answer, and divide the one from the other?*

The day after Christmas it began to snow in the afternoon. The snow fell softly over the darkening vale and lay in thick drifts across the farthest deeps. Fine like chalk, it fell briskly in narrow swirls into the windless night. A crystal night made up of glass objects. The purity, the stillness, the inner beauty of things shone forth. I did not go to bed and kept watching the quick efficient flakes softly falling through those endless realms. At dawn it stopped snowing, and the sky, gray and overcast, began to clear. I dozed off in my armchair and dreamt of my father. But upon waking I remembered nothing of the dream. Only my sight, hovering between sleep and awareness, was arrested by a branch of the cottonwood near the window that had in its long, knotted fingers unwittingly caught a passing cloud.

III

'. . . U.S.S.R. Or let us be direct and courteous for once. The United States Socialist Republic,' came the swift mocking voice from behind. Swift and cultured and elevated sounding, as if the speaker was high up on a rostrum somewhere.

'Not totally there yet,' the man's back was nearly touching mine, 'but not much far either. When things get too dear, people barter their freedoms in a hurry. And that is exactly what is going to happen. It hardly mattered how much worthless money they pressed into our hands while we were holed up in our homes. But now we are starting to come out and all hell is about to break loose. It's inevitable, Giulia, run the figures however you like. The charts look horrible, and the numbers are worse each day.'

'The cold beauty of numbers,' chimed in the woman opposite him. I had walked past her only moments ago. Her figure had looked a little too heavy for her sharp blue dress and those classy black stilettos that instantly drew your eye to them. But the dress and the shoes told you that Giulia had once been very pretty and was quite proud of it and that dressing this way came naturally to her.

'Cold, hard, utterly inflexible,' the man sent the trite remark spinning into the air with a flick of his fingers. 'Unyielding just when you need a bit of wiggle room. Nipping every good intention in the bud. Ask any kind-hearted politician who desires simply to do right by his voters. And, here in New York, aren't they all kind-hearted?'

The delicate ebb and flow of sarcasm lent the voice a prophetic air. It lifted the simple words into an eerie realm where one foreboding touched another across the quickening mists of time. I saw further than I would have otherwise seen, as if by way of a sixth sense, which absorbed all my impressions and made them fluid.

And parting these mists, cutting through the airport traffic on the turnpike, came forth the yellow taxi. Cattails to my left waved in the breeze and opened out in a westerly crescent under the afternoon sun. A gentle massing of clouds was slowly approaching the city from the north. Then at the turn, the oddly diminutive skyline of Manhattan, which had been visible here and there beyond the tight rocks to my right, was suddenly ahead of us, now quite big and imposing. I saw again those empty rail tracks, shining like so many silver streams in a bed of rust, fill the earth with a mood of sad neglect. Further off, where they appeared to vanish into a vast unseen pit, rose heavenward the sleek and efficient towers, jammed close and reflecting a subdued, other-worldly light.

I felt I had been specially chosen and brought here by some secret will, far stronger than my own, to bear witness to the end of an era, the gradual fritting away of power, prestige, and prosperity to the point of no return, the fate of all empires, which the scene before me seemed to portend in all its haunting grandeur.

'Know how much they printed since they locked this place down last spring?' the refined voice cut through my rising vertigo. 'More than half the currency in circulation. Others give a higher figure, as high as eighty percent. See what I mean? They're never going to stop. Slow down every now and then maybe. But pause completely? No. Never. They simply cannot. The entire mess will explode in their face.'

Not in serene vertiginous buildings but in people themselves do we find, if we are careful and alert to the mood of the moment, the clearest sense of an ending.

Time had resumed its course, but I felt as if some great learning had descended upon me. Ideas and images that had for long lain scattered in different corners of my mind, fell into place with surprising readiness. With slow, deliberate movement, I shifted to the chair on my right. I could now properly see my speakers, even hear them better, for I could still hear perfectly from my left ear. I didn't want to miss a thing.

'The die was cast a long time ago,' the man carried on calmly. 'Twelve years or twenty, does it matter? Back in the Nineties, when LTCM blew up and the Street bailed them out, I used to wonder what they'd do the second time. Who would save these banks in the next crisis? And we got our answer in o-eight, Giulia, didn't we? All you have got to do, I said to myself at the time, is to wait a little. All you have got to do, Richard, is to let the entire sorry affair play out. Who could've imagined they'd be able to stave it off for this long? Of course, the more we delay, the more terrible will be the reckoning. Much worse than Zimbabwe or Venezuela, for at least they don't go on flooding the world with their worthless paper.'

'And yet, by some miracle, the world can't have enough of our money,' countered the woman. 'The more we print, the more it seems to have a need for.'

'We have created a Frankenstein's monster that will end up swallowing us whole.'

'Out there is an infinite demand for dollars, Richard,' she continued. 'Any tightening of liquidity instantly shows you who is king. We saw that as soon as countries started to shut down. Even I was surprised by the quickness of it, by what I saw coming, and just how good the returns might be if I was careful. This when I'd been keeping a close eye on Eurodollar futures since the curve inversion in June of Eighteen. The profits, as it turned out, were even better in the FX swaps market.'

A certain pride shone through her response. The man did not seem to mind it. He remained silent and did not contradict her. I had the impression that inside that large head of his was a small Bloomberg-style terminal busily processing data flows and conducting complex analyses.

'Out there maybe, but in here too?' he finally let go of his inertia. 'You, my dear, are conflating two very different issues. At least, in terms of the repercussions that would immediately follow. Yes, the entire system is underpinned by the mighty dollar and, for this reason alone, is extremely fragile in my opinion. Any one of the many black swans floating around can cause it to unwind in a matter of weeks. This hyper financialized global economy built upon endlessly borrowing from the future is one credit event away from contagion and collapse. When that happens who stands to lose the most? The thought itself is terrifying.

'Money needs to run like water through the plumbing for the system to function smoothly. For to have a reserve currency of the first rank means little more than to have for it a deep and liquid bond market, yes? Everywhere and always, dollars should flow easily. No shock of any kind can be allowed to occur. After all, the world works on energy, whose uninterrupted availability is the very basis of civilization, or what precious little remains of it. To buy this energy, if nothing else, you need our money. And you sure as hell need our money for much besides. Out there, no doubt, is an infinite demand for dollars, which also entails that a strong dollar is in no one's interest. A rising dollar will break this monetary setup faster than a falling one. And a falling one most certainly will. We can neither let it strengthen nor suffer it to weaken. This ordinarily is what you'd call a checkmate. A player approaching such a circumstance would sooner throw up their hands and resign than face complete and utter humiliation. But it's likely that not many care for chess on Pennsylvania or Constitution Avenue, in scenic Arlington or in the trading pits of Wall Street. Either that or they know something we don't.'

'They know that it's much worse in other places.'

He seemed to have not heard her.

'For far too long,' he continued, 'those who rule in our name have neglected those of us who put them there in the first place, each time sacrificing our interests at the altar of their dangerous delusions, this absurd wish to continue their global hegemony by whatever means necessary. They have bankrupted us in the process and earned us enemies in every corner of the globe, to say nothing of the bodies that have been steadily stacking up since Vietnam. Nearly everything our leaders do makes a mockery of the guarantees enshrined in the Bill of Rights and the founding spirit behind this once great republic. They cause money to magically appear at the push of a button and exchange it for real, tangible stuff the rest of the world is only too happy to sell us. Everyone needs our dollars! Of course, this decimates jobs and lowers living standards, fermenting trouble, and splitting the nation further. Look at the anxiety and anguish spreading far and wide, while our minders grow rich doing precisely nothing. The most affluent counties in America today are within fifty miles of our capital. Now ask yourself exactly what is it that Washington manufactures that it should grow so wealthy so quickly.

'We've erected a mammoth phony economy over and above a shrinking real one, where more and more gains accrue to a handful of people, while they deign to put in the mail for the rest of us thousand-dollar relief checks each quarter. Then they step out into the sun and make a fuss about wealth gaps and trade deficits. Smoke and mirrors, I tell you— and underneath that: old man Triffin's horrid dilemma. Nixon learnt it the hard way. We too may do so very soon. Except that this time there won't be any fire escapes open to hurry through.'

The words had come in a rush though somehow each word was given its proper due. The man's persona was unnaturally calm, as if he had seen the future from a long way off and cultivated patience at great personal cost. His little speech had me in thrall. I was fully attentive, unable to tear myself away. Partly, it was a matter of cadence, although who will deny that it is nice to hear now and then the concern of the moneyed for the average fellow on the street. How quietly disarming it is to find someone of that set, far removed from the general precarity of life, throw in his lot with the rest of us, the unschooled and the uninformed, rushing headlong into the raging tempest.

Across the alley in the dappled shade two men were in fact playing chess. Frozen as statues, they pondered the crowded space in the middle. I could just about place the pieces on the nearest side. Something moved in the opposite ranks and the next moment a black bishop stood in b4, close but safe for the time being from the white knights in c3 and d4. In the diagonal separating the bishop from the knights were two white and two black pawns. The pawns looked ripe for an exchange, and the white's queen and rooks further down looked sharp and hungry for attack. A storm was brewing near the bottom of the board.

'They'll find a way,' said the woman after a pause. 'They always do. The entire thing is made up anyway. Fiat trading against fiat. Who could've imagined it just fifty years ago! Yet billions of dollars change hands each day based on just such an arrangement. When they perform a reset and usher in a brand-new regime, everyone everywhere will fall in line. We still have our navy, don't we? The greatest armada on the face of the earth backs our currency.'

'And what backs this formidable navy? It is circular reasoning. A logical fallacy that won't hold out for long. The next crisis will start a chain of sovereign defaults that will reach our shores earlier than we may think.'

'Technically speaking,' replied the woman, 'we can't go bankrupt. Technically speaking, our creditors can always be reimbursed in full.' She now sounded only half serious.

The man gave a low chuckle. 'But how?' he asked rhetorically. 'With fresh unlimited supplies of fiat? Each new bill worth less than the previous one, with nothing behind it but the empty guarantee of an insolvent, profiteer state. There comes a time when technicalities alone are not enough. Yet I do not doubt for a moment that is precisely what they're going to try. Form over substance. Governments are rather good at it.'

'They won't be left with much choice in the matter. And maybe this is the plan. When things go south, people will ask for all kinds of subsidies and welfare spends,' she finally appeared to be agreeing with him. 'If one government fails to honor their demands, they'll vote themselves another bunch that will. Who can blame them when every politician points to this very potential of democracy? Greatest good for the greatest number! Nothing like an emergency to test the truth of a statement. Of course, past our borders the issues will be altogether of a different cast and magnitude.

'It'd behoove them, you'd think, to get in front of the problem while there's still time.' She was getting ready to practice her own brand of irony. 'My advice to the clever folk in Washington would be to skip the whole charade and merge the Treasury with the Fed right away. Streamline the process for when you have to put your money where your mouth is. Straight into people's pockets that is. And I mean real money, not the puny sums we were offered last year.'

'A journey of a thousand steps begins with the first, or so observed the sage from China once upon a time. Which is only to say that our great leaders have heard your wish. Take the recent CARES Act, for example. Virtually overnight they created a Treasury fund of half a trillion dollars to be put into the Fed's emergency facilities. Smooth operators, the lot of them! The names they come up with! Most of this money will end up in the markets one way or another, presumedly to plug leaks and stop this financial Titanic from keeling over. If that isn't in pursuit of public good most manifestly, I don't know what is.'

He was clearly enjoying himself.

'The trouble with these people is that they can't be bothered to think even medium term. Two years is their absolute outer limit. No one sees the writing on the wall. And if they never see the inevitable, how can they prepare for it? Meanwhile, with each election cycle, the inevitable is a whole lot closer. Our debt is off the charts, the unfunded liabilities run into hundreds of trillions, and the economy is so hooked on cheap money that a modest rate rise will push it right over the cliff. Pull the drug bowl away for a minute and watch the addict go into acute paroxysms! Just imagine a scenario where the rates have to rise by a mere five hundred basis points. Not a lot if inflation is consistently running at nine or ten percent, which seems a foregone conclusion given the climate we find ourselves in—a climate, dare I say, of increasing velocity and recurring supply shocks. How long before the entire federal debt becomes unserviceable? And what then? Will they hastily abandon their hawkish stance and start to ease back in a high inflationary environment and risk becoming another Weimar Germany, or will they continue to tighten and precipitate a global depression worse than the Thirties? The answer should be obvious to anyone. Yet no matter what path they take, no matter what kind of government people put into office, the result won't be any different. On the one hand, larger and larger dollar loans and swaps will be needed to grease the global monetary machine and keep it functional; on the other, an easy policy here at home will suppress yields for longer, creating yet more indebtedness and inflation for years on end. Price discovery will be over for good, and the Fed's balance sheet will keep expanding in perpetuity or until they have taken direct or indirect ownership of every financial asset or security in the world. Naturally, this means that our government will have to get much bigger, most of its time spent in passing new expanded regulations and annulling old modest ones. Thousands of pages of legalese that no one will care to read or know how to. Day by day, hour by hour, we will slip into a command economy with all its attending benefits: mass nationalizations, shortages, and price controls. A model Orwellian state will appear to have arisen almost organically. Like it or not, you will get your soviet-style politburo and a country full of serfs.'

A dark, troubling vision with a note of high tragedy. He had built a strong case over several minutes of what was to unfold in the coming years. It was as good a place as any to stop, but he still had a little left to say.

'It's a myth to call these markets free. There haven't been any for years. Just see the total impunity with which Central Banks operate everywhere, how they disregard even the most basic rules of the game, printing with one hand and buying with the other. It's a magic trick, a shadow play to divert the children from the horrors gathering behind their backs. As is quite well known, the Bank of Japan today holds more than fifty percent of all publicly issued government debt. There you have it, the hoped for fiscal and monetary union! It's effectively killed the bond market. Days go by without anything catching a bid. Not satisfied with this though, the Bank has also steadily acquired around half a trillion dollars of Japanese equities. Its balance sheet is higher than Japan's gross domestic product. Does this look like free market capitalism to you? But forget reversing course, there's no sign of even slowing down. This is basically where we are all headed. In London and Frankfurt, in Beijing and Washington, they eye the Japanese experiment with awe and envy. When these people speak, the tone deafness is staggering. Just thinking of the future makes one's stomach turn. We are about to get a lot poorer, Giulia, both materially and spiritually.'

'Call it the Schumpeter wager then,' she improvised, trying to shift the mood a little. 'You don't need blood in the streets, loud fanatics, or class struggle, says Professor Schumpeter. What you need is quite simply more capitalist innovation, which, in the present context, can only mean more financial innovation. Follow the lead of history, let corporatism and creative destruction run out their course, and before long you will find yourself crossing the Rubicon into fabulous socialism.'

'Or fascism,' the man's tone was suddenly grave. 'At my age, it's often hard to tell the difference. Either way, you'd do well to be far from here when that happens. Far away and off the grid. Self-sufficient, relying on no one but your closest friends and family. Change at such scale is never peaceful and rarely leads to a benign utopia. That is a pipe dream academics think up in their cool, ivied moments.'

'Neo-feudalism, more likely,' I said under my breath. Back to the twelfth century with tools of the twenty-first. The terrifying acceleration of technology favoring none but the very few, making past models of reasoning flawed or deficient. Almost daily one heard of awkward young men with messiah complexes raising huge sums in the name of bringing the future to the world's depressed and marginalized; sums that instead ended up feeding new advanced chains and algorithms which fuzzed up the psyche in unpredictable ways. And now the algorithms themselves were on the verge of turning sentient. The disruption to come, the disruption already taking place in the public sphere, had no parallel in history. Soon it would be like a geological force transforming every aspect of life. From the Anthropocene into the Algocene! The case the stranger had built over the last few minutes felt logical and necessary but also somehow outdated. Human ideas for a human world, built upon human emotions and human judgments. Could such misplaced notions prepare one for a future of extreme unpredictable outcomes?

The man was reluctant to speak further. I would have liked to put to him one or two questions of my own. But how? Even without asking, I had been granted a certain vision, a gift of knowledge I didn't know I needed. It was more than I could have imagined barely an hour ago when stepping out of the dim cool interior of the famous library I had come looking for something to eat. Into the glare of the day, I had moved amid the summer throng, landing finally a spot on the busy promenade sheltered by the tall London Planes that make up the northern end of Bryant Park along Forty Second.

Sensing that the conversation had run its course, the two began to speak of lighter matters. I heard something about going to dinner at The Yale Club on East Forty-Fourth once the last panel for the day had concluded.

Who were these people? Professors on tour? Shocked and incensed libertarians? Bond vigilantes readying their next act? The last grieving descendants of the Austrian School? If I could chance upon a discussion like this at the edge of a small city park while out at lunch, it followed that others too were seriously debating these topics in clubs and boardrooms all over the island. Not in New York alone, but in Chicago, LA, Miami, countless actors were thinking and preparing for just such an extreme and turbulent eventuality. And what was taking place across the length and breadth of America was surely not being ignored by the wider world.

I, myself, was not entirely unschooled in economics; what was more, I had cut my teeth long ago working as a lawyer in capital markets. Vague, abstract ideas I had entertained once, the passage of time had filled up and made concrete and knotty. But the world had not stayed still either. It had turned simultaneously into a dull and dangerous place. Fifteen years earlier, in the prime of my youth, I had seen in London the debt-fueled affluence reminiscent of the Roaring Twenties. Now here in the heart of corporate America was I to be given an alternative experience? In a country I had grown to love despite its challenges, had the moment finally arrived for a macabre and spectacular unwinding of decades of excess and bacchanalia?

The new Twenties, I thought, may well turn out to be the old Thirties.

On the board across the alley, the storm had come and gone. Bishops, knights, and pawns had vanished in the thick of the fray. And the white king, castled and secure until recently, lay mated in its black square. The players were silent, mentally going over the last moves; their backs, drenched in sweat, showed in the sea of their shirts.

The two strangers to my left were chatting casually, but I could barely hear them now. It was as if they were far away, conversing in the language of birds. The park was teeming with people. A warm hum rose from it and up through the well of the buildings and vanished into the clear Manhattan sky. Here and there, you caught a stray glance in a masked face—the wariness of being close to others after having remained indoors for so long. The walkways and sections around the stalls and the carrousel were filled with voices and laughter like before, and on Sixth Avenue, emptier than usual, the cars went by very fast toward the wall of trees in the distance. In the open space behind me, reclining in chairs or sprawled on the grass, men, women, and children carried on unsuspectingly, happy to be in the sun again after the stress and anxiety of the past year. At the other end of the park, the dark, gothic drama of the American Radiator Building lay hidden behind screens and scaffoldings. Only the beveled, geometric crown and the surrounding friezes were free of any covering. They glittered a solid gold in the harsh July blaze. Even after a hundred years, the dare Raymond Hood had thrown his fellow practitioners had not been bettered.

It was impossible to return to the library and continue my reading after what I had heard. I finished my coffee and began to walk home. Opposite St. Patrick's, I stumbled upon my steps from three years ago: the busy, humid sidewalk cutting across block upon block of tall buildings, a leaden sky stuck between them, rose before my stinging eyes. My very first time in the city, streaks of color in the summer rain and the moon over East River; the many shimmering towers in the distance releasing a false sentiment of homecoming. Three full years separated me from that bit of fuchsia which had hung in the air a moment like some forgotten fragrance as the girl in front had turned left into the Plaza.

Although we now had a home here, both Rita and I still behaved like outsiders. We had never quite adjusted to the place, and Rita often spoke longingly of our first year in the valley, our own private idyll, which, having come so unexpectedly, had turned out to be so short lived. She felt this loss deeply and lamented the fact that she couldn't go back there every week like I did when the classes were in session. For at the start of our second summer, Rita had been offered a role at a big pension fund headquartered in the City, and before we knew it, the two of us found ourselves, out of breath and at our wits' end, in the great stony upheaval of Manhattan.

But the idyll—such being the nature of idylls—was not meant to last. And yet, miraculously somehow, it had lasted an entire year. And the year had been strange and magical, in tune with the music of the seasons. A period of renewal, of gradual replenishment of strength and hope. Maybe it was for the better that the spell was broken. Better that we hadn't had the time to grow used to the relaxed life together, that we were taken out of it before every new experience had become merely a memory and a habit of the old. It had been a timeless world of romance, a kind of second childhood in the country, where simply a glance, step, or gesture could unlock an epiphany.

I walked some blocks further, then turned east on Fifty-Seventh. A few minutes later, looking down Lex, I saw a lone cloud flying from the spire of the Chrysler like a shining standard above the roof of a mythic pagoda, the familiar parabolic dome with its terraced steel arches, triangular windows, and sunbursts radiating as if from an invisible source within.

It would have been nice to get behind those windows and watch the summer light set parts of the Hudson on fire. Once it was indeed possible to do so for as little as fifty cents. Inside the crown, there had been an observatory, a space dominated by strong lines and curves, that was shut down in the Forties. The sole black and white photo I had seen in one of the books in the library showed orbs hanging from the ceiling at precise intervals with stars gleaming past them from the vaulted shadows. The celestial theme was carried on to the walls that were decorated with large sunburst patterns to create a sense of homogeneity. As without so within. It was dizzying to read in the present, more than nine decades later, about the skill and daring, the extraordinary efficiency and craftsmanship, of the people who had help raise inside of two years this much-loved New York icon seventy-seven floors into the sky. Did not the large striking mural Edward Trumbull had painted above the main concourse celebrate just this fact? Human will and ingenuity channeling the brute forces of nature into streamlined modern wonders. The confidence of that generation, much like the promise of its emergent technologies, seemed entirely limitless.

Up in the dome, the sun, the clouds, a hint of the flaming sea; music of the spheres and eagles setting out in four directions. While down below, treasures quarried from Morocco, Sienna, and Mexico; red marble, banded onyx, and yellow travertine shining in the glow of Nirosta reflectors that brushed the air a soft amber. Beauty in harmony encased in the richness of color: every detail and motif was calibrated for maximum effect. There had been many starts previously, soaring attempts by ambitious men to render in stone the distinct mood of the moment. But it was only here, at the junction of Lexington Avenue and Forty-Second Street, that Deco, or the triumphal expression of a heterogenous modernity dangerously close to collapse, was first properly established in the public imagination.

Yes, it held its own even now, one and ninety years after the fact, in the heavily crenelated sky of Manhattan, the realization of a dream far beyond the comprehension of ordinary men by ordinary standards.

In truth, I was as much enamored with the building as with its architect, William Van Alen. The Chrysler had been the glory and the ruin of this taciturn and singular man. He should have been a model for every artist, for he had done something many wish for, but few end up achieving: to vanish completely into your creation. A lesson in humility and fortitude, and an inspiration for a soul at the crossroads of his creative journey. When during the Depression years his commissions steadily declined—thanks in no small part to a suit he had instituted against the owner of the building, Walter Percy Chrysler, for the recovery of monies owed to him and which the automobile tycoon refused to pay in the absence of a written contract—Van Alen gradually distanced himself from his old profession and became a teacher of sculpture. It was not a decision made from any bitterness, at least not outwardly so. For although he never help build another skyscraper, he did, through the Thirties, work on several small innovative ideas, among them a plan to manufacture prefabricated steel houses for the working class. Nine years before his death at the age of seventy-one, Van Alen was elected a member of the National Academy of Design. Yet his passage from the scene (like his model for a 'House of the Modern Age', displayed at the corner of Park and Thirty-Ninth and disassembled six months later) had left no residue. For someone whose creation had become a symbol of an age and was admired around the world, it was remarkable how little I had been able to find during my research about this period of his life.

Off Second Avenue, under the striped marquee of the pre-war boutique building, the white-gloved doorman was holding back for me the long shiny brass door pull. Beyond the threshold was a world miles away from the noisy street. From the iron tendrils spreading over the glass doors to the Edgar Brandt designed lamps and detailing throwing a muffled light on the smooth bluestone floors, the expensive lobby transported you back a hundred years into a quite understated kind of Deco elegance.

I rode the teak-paneled elevator to my apartment on the fourteenth floor. From the living room you could see clear across Upper East Side all the way to East Harlem. I watched the red cable car glide above the traffic on Queensboro Bridge and vanish behind the gray structure to my left. I waited and sipped my tea. It came back more crowded this time, arms flailing in every window, and headed for the river.

In the evening, Rita was happy to find me at home after nearly a fortnight. She called me into the bedroom to unzip her dress. Years had hardly touched her frame. She was still the same lean girl I had first known in college. She dropped her underwear on the floor and began telling me about her workday. She was seldom troubled by my gaze. It was as if we had long been set free of that type of desire for one another. When she was safely in the shower, I asked her what her colleagues thought about the economy and the markets. Did they, for instance, see any cause for concern or alarm? I tried to remember more of the conversation I had heard at lunch.

'Why, the US remains the best place to invest in the medium term. The markets here have outperformed most other markets over the last decade. And nobody sees this trend reversing anytime soon, not with the current macro set anyway.'

So the man had not been wrong. The optimism was widespread and skin-deep. It was perhaps time to start worrying a little. I said nothing and began to go out.

'By the way,' her voice rose above the sound of water, 'I bought my first Ether yesterday.'

'Good lord!' I murmured under my breath, closing the bathroom door behind me. I had the feeling she had heard me and was smiling contentedly.

We could still give each other satisfaction, did still react along expected lines. In the bedroom windows the red tramway went by silently across the now dark shimmering towers.

Friday was my day off. I awoke after Rita had already left for work. I had no wish to go anywhere or see anyone or eat anything, so I read until half past one in the airconditioned quiet of the flat. Down in the ravine, sirens wailed above the traffic rush. Around four, I dozed off listening to a night raga by Shruti Sadolikar, queen among singers, and dreamt of moonlight over a forested hill. When I next stirred in my sleep, I heard Rita talking to someone in the other room. Half-conscious, I wondered if it was Rosamund. Then I realized she wasn't due in New York until a week later.

But it was her voice alright. I came awake at once. The two were engaged in a discussion on altcoins of all things. '. . .yes, Ethereum, and, recently, I maxed out on Solana and Dogecoin too!' beamed Rosamund with genuine pleasure. 'Now imagine if the price moved up just one decimal place! Think of the returns! *These are still early days.*'

'And what if the price jumps two or three places? What will we do then?' Rita teased her, probably beginning to dream herself.

These are still early days! One had started to hear this line a lot since some of the big money from the Street had moved in to put all that government stimulus to work. *Crypto sisters early on the trade,* I thought lightly. A revolution led by savvy women buying up strings of numbers on a blockchain. Anything was possible in a world of cheap debt and unlimited fiat. Sooner or later, someone was going to get hurt.

It was pleasant to linger in bed and hear more of their conversation filtering through the walls. I thought back to the time these two had first met. A jazz night in Theater District. Ron Carter at Birdland leading a twenty-piece ensemble in his eighty-second year on earth. What better rendezvous could be imagined? Rosamund had been dating this girl from Tunisia, ten years her junior. They looked dazzling together, two graceful beings arrived this minute from some faraway planet, bodies carefully and delicately sculpted as if by an old, masterly hand. An ache, made of equal parts physical and nonphysical causes, rose in my chest. I didn't know I still had it in me to feel this way. But a sudden concentration of feminine beauty had been known to drive men mad. A quick visceral response to the perfection of form. Was it all this simple? Was desire merely a matter of biology? Of a slight agitation in the blood? And had she too, out of her womanly intuition, felt my confusion and need? Was this why she held on to me longer than was necessary, enough anyway to have made Rita wary?

'For Gina,' Rosamund had said out loud moving away. The doll in the pleated skirt stood on the side and smiled serenely, patiently waiting for the introduction.

Rita thought Rosamund was referring to my late friend. But Rosamund had spoken the name like a quip or a private joke. And then I made the connection. It was not a real but a fictional person she had in mind: Contessa Gina Pietranera, later the Duchess Sanseverina, in Stendhal's famous novel *La Chartreuse de Parme*. 'Never before or after in literature,' I had said to her on one of those inspired nights in the mountains years ago, 'have I encountered a moment more emotionally pure than the one where the Duchess embraces her nephew, the youthful and facile Fabrice del Dongo, upon his return from Waterloo. To this day, I can feel the charge and warmth of that embrace.'

'She's in love with you,' Rita had said to me later at home. I was struck by her complete lack of sentimentality.

'Yes, but not how you think. Plus, she adores that girl.'

'Who? That doll? Don't be silly. They won't last six months.'

The evening was melting in the windows of the gray tower across the street. I managed to pull myself out of bed and went into the living room. Rosamund jumped from the sofa. It was nice to feel this burst of warmth in the apartment. She said she was already halfway in New Haven before it occurred to her to come a week early and surprise us. We decided to walk to the park and then go somewhere to eat. A half hour later we were in the Sheep Meadow. Once on the West Side, we strolled along Amsterdam Avenue until we found a place we liked.

We came back skirting the reservoir into which night had properly fallen. The lit towers of El Dorado on Central Park West lay upside down in the water. At the bottom of the steps near South Gate House a small crowd had collected. This group of late walkers stood around a refuse bin, arms out and phones on the ready, talking in hushed tones and watching a red fox whose hunger had momentarily got the better of its shyness.

'What happened?' Rosamund asked me.

'Why, nothing.' I lied.

Outside the Met, we hailed a cab and were home in ten minutes. Sunday Rosamund left for Providence and on Monday I was back in the valley.

Classes were now in full swing and with each passing day I had less and less desire to return to the city. Some weeks I didn't go back at all; other times, Rita came up from New York to spend the weekend in the country. During such visits, we pretended that nothing had changed, that there was no other life but this, that our private idyll was still intact. On the balcony, in remembrance of things past, the moon and the wind released a silver rustle from the birches, while very late at night, the murmur of the stream was sharp and clear through my insomnia.

One evening longing to inhabit a mind far removed from my own, longing to be put in touch with an older, simpler way of life, I retreated into the ancient solitude of Wang Wei's poetry, perfect words that reached me from across a chasm of twelve centuries. After I was finished with Wang Wei, I read some Izumi Shikibu, and recalled lines from a poem by Jane Hirshfield, translator of Shikibu's daring verse. When I opened my eyes, a full moon was rising inside the heavenly proscenium, throwing its halo on the curtain of clouds around it. Dark as retreating bison, a large vapor trail flew across this glowing vertical plane. *There are openings in our lives*, I said under my breath,

> *of which we know nothing.*
> *Through them*
> *the belled herds travel at will,*
> *long-legged and thirsty, covered with foreign dust.*

The mist of harebells on the heath died slowly, and the blue hour of eventide signaled an end to summer. By and by the last of the glaciers quietly melted and the landscape of memory turned bare and scraggly.

But then the weather began to cool, and spots of color started to show in places. Green hills were touched by passing clouds and where the clouds lifted there appeared amid the verdure bright dots of red and yellow. Another fall entered the earth, another miracle crept upon us. I reminisced about that autumn in Kashmir which had been the harbinger of many catastrophes. Soon it was fall no more but winter. Color faded like the hours and the skies turned gray and heavy. In between the seasons, unrest broke out in several cities. Scenes of looting and vandalism flashed on television sets night after night. Shops went up in flames in the wintry darkness and civic buildings faced the brunt of people's ire. For a while, marches and rioting and clashes with the police became all too common. The damage from arson alone crossed one billion dollars. In the papers, editors drew cautious parallels with the Sixties. Birth of a new consciousness, they declaimed. A culture of change and justice and equity was finally here to right past wrongs. To me, in some respects still an outsider, the mood looked decidedly premodern even if couched in up-to-date radical terminology. It was the mood of a Serge or a Dostoyevsky, of the India of my childhood, rife with social and economic fault lines. When one paid attention, the talk circulating in every corner was a talk of inconsistencies and platitudes. This was a young Chateaubriand describing the Paris in the months before the Revolution, but he could as well have been speaking of my own neighborhood. I quickly learned not to draw such comparisons, for they annoyed my listeners and made them impatient. It was a form of American exceptionalism in action. The impatience told you that you were foolish to think in historical terms, that the American condition was unique just like the American experiment had been unique, that these things could not happen here.

And clearly, this wasn't Czarist or Stalinist Russia, nor the Ancien Régime convulsing uncontrollably in its death throes. This was America, caretaker of the world, and possessing an unlimited power of fiat. Hence, the government simply wrote off the losses and waited for the anger to cool over. When the worst had passed, it did what it knew best: throw money at the problem with both hands.

Money was given and money was used up. It scarcely mattered anyway as long as foreigners were buying our debt by the fistfuls. But the world could see what was unfolding. Hollowed out from the inside, the empire was contracting. In Asian dailies, opinion pieces announced the end of *Pax Americana* and the duplicitous regime it had fostered, a merciful belated end to the tyranny and caprice of America incapable of putting even its own house in order. And yet, contrary to expectations, the dollar did not break, did not make a new low. For a brief period, it traded in a tight band, then started to consolidate and strengthen.

Each time something happened, each time nothing happened, I remembered the conversation I had heard by chance earlier in the summer. How long, I wondered, before something truly cracked? How long before the entire system, teetering on the edge, came undone in a rude and vulgar fashion? History that I had read in books or seen on film was now like a persistent thud in the ear. It screeched from the rails of the subway and rang in the bells of cathedrals and exchanges. Through the murmur of crowds, it flowed toward the open sea; and down the tops of unfinished buildings, it stared at you from the numerous derricks knotting the city's skyline.

But will America preserve its form of government? Will the States not sunder? Chateaubriand had pondered the very question two hundred years ago. The Romans had held on to a collapsing empire for centuries. Could we not do the same? And yet, what had once taken years to accomplish, was now handled in a matter of minutes. *So long as liberty produces gold, an industrial republic performs wonders.* But gold had been dubbed an ancient relic and taken off the charts, and the industry, long since shuttered and broken up, had been sold to the highest bidder.

In the Eighteen Thirties, when industry was in its nascency and much of America still pastoral, the English-born American artist Thomas Cole had created a series of five paintings for his patron, the New York merchant Luman Reed. *The Course of Empire* presented a cyclical view of history that borrowed ideas from the works of Byron and Gibbon and placed them inside romantic Hudson Valley landscapes. It was a vision of the future starkly different from that of his contemporaries. Describing the fifth and final painting titled 'Desolation', Cole, perhaps unknowingly, echoed the feelings of Chateaubriand when he observed: 'Violence and time have crumbled the works of man, and art is again resolving into elemental nature. The gorgeous pageant has passed—the roar of battle has ceased—the multitude has sunk in the dust—the empire is extinct.'

'I would like to have a child. I don't want to grow old alone with you.'

'What's got into you? Have you looked outside lately? No one need suffer more than is necessary.'

'Don't be dramatic. This is New York not Kathmandu. Millions would kill for an opportunity to be here.'

'In Kathmandu, on the contrary, I might even have considered.'

She is furious, but her eyes are wet. She turns away and switches off the lamp.

'I want a child,' her voice, barely audible this time, reaches me from the depths of the night. I must steel myself for the both of us. When the weakness has passed, she will thank me for it. Or she will blame me for her loneliness in the years to come.

The year so recently begun was already waning. The world seemed to have slipped into a stasis—a kind of coma in which one passed from day to day and thought nothing of the future. At the base of the great towers, a mood of desolation reigned at dusk. It was as if no sun had ever touched those walls, as if they had just emerged from an ocean of slime. I felt this acutely each time I walked down Lex, pulled in that direction almost against my will by the glowing dome of the Chrysler.

Around Thanksgiving, Herman called to tell me he had just returned from a holiday in Kashmir. There was so much color, he said, it had driven Niki mad. The snow peaks, higher and lighter than clouds, hung like a mirage at the edge of vision. They had reminded him of my father. Speaking to Herman put me at ease. He always had that effect on me. Toward the evening, I finally sat down to reply to Kalan's last mail, which I had been putting off for the better part of a month. In a few weeks, he would turn eighty. A solitary old man in a remote corner of the Himalaya.

On the last day of classes, walking to the campus stop, I passed a row of ginkgo trees that had almost overnight shed all their leaves. The yellow fan-shaped thing had the weight of deep time. It spoke of an older geological age, millions of years before the first humans, a period when earth was not the earth we knew but a different, alien planet. The veins in the leaf didn't interlock like every other species this side of the glacial thaw but branched out in widening arcs of ease and expansiveness. Between my fingers was a perfectly preserved quantum of past aeons. It made me breathless. When the bus arrived, I noticed that the young privet bush at my knee was drenched in birdsong.

That night I had a curious dream. I was driving along the wooded bank of a lake under a crescent moon. It could have been any of the lakes I had visited during my lifetime. Any of the countless Himalayan lakes, or one of those glistening turquoise bodies in the Southern Alps. It might even have been Windermere or Derwentwater. Yet somehow I had the impression that it was Lake George and no other and that it had a connection to Cole, painter of landscapes and the decline of empires. I was driving in pitch dark, for no light came down through the trees. Someone had switched the banks. The left was right and the right left. Suddenly the road turned, and I lost control. The car swerved and fell into the lake. Slowly, it sank through infinite space. Water began to pour in from the opening in the windowpane. Pinned to my seat, I was unable to free myself. In panic, in desperation, I struggled. But it was futile. I had to let go. At once, my attention shifted to the one who was dying, he who was not me, he who was made wholly of the elements. The water now felt lighter than the night. It magnified the stars and brought them closer. They filled the sky from end to end, magnificently and utterly. In time, I went toward them.

Something substantial had taken place, a kind of dream initiation, a strange astral death and a profound awakening. The next day passed in a beatific daze. *Dvija*, or twice born, the *Rig Veda* had called the sacrificial fire. And this fire had purified me, granting a glimpse into the self that was neither body nor mind. A new self, or a second self with a new awareness.

There were still things I wished to say, things that needed saying. A form would be needed to speak the unsayable, but a form would grow along with the words. I remembered my arrival in the valley at the height of summer. From the window, I could see lone dark clouds drifting east, outlined a deep orange by the last of the sun. High above, the sky was the color of slate, except where the shroud had thinned and given these oblong patches a curious mauve flush.

A blue jay was scolding in the river birch.

At Bliss Mountain

'Gir is dead.'

By the time Rosamund called from New York to give me the shocking news, Niki had already left me. Thirty stories below, the streets were flooded, and the lights of stranded cars all the way to the Sea Link were impressionist smudges on the glass. Out over the darkness of Arabian Sea, rain hung like a curtain. Cyclones in March were rare, but soon it would be April when cyclones were not so uncommon. Yet they were already calling this the wettest spring in decades. Further south, the rains had been continuous for more than two weeks, and the dams, built on seasonal rivers as a hedge against droughts, were on the point of bursting. Who could forget those scenes of devastation and horror from three summers ago? Twice in my sleep, I had seen the bottom half of the continent in a state of perpetual dissolution.

I had been in no mood to join the long traffic snarl to the empty flat on the other side of that bridge. Nobody would miss me there. Niki had taken the cats with her. Niki had finally made the decision that was always hers to make.

'He drove for an hour to somewhere outside Woodstock,' Rosamund tried especially hard to keep an even tone. The connection kept dropping every few minutes. My feet felt cold and free of blood. Each heartbeat was a hammer blow in the ear.

There was a Buddhist monastery on the side of a hill that Gir had discovered quite by accident. Its head lama, younger than him, had been born in Eastern Tibet. Gir had once watched this monk direct a ceremonial initiation with aplomb. 'Nine hundred years of lineage on those narrow, red-robed shoulders,' he had said to me. A quarter mile from the monastery grounds was a clearing where people left their cars to go for hikes into the mountain. Further ahead, a stream rushed beneath a wooden footbridge past which, to the left of the path, was a stand of aspens. It was a spot Gir knew well and had come to love deeply. He would go there when the mood came upon him.

I had been told about the place, had heard all about the peace of the aspens above the cascading water. But it was only now, as Rosamund spoke, that I saw it clearly for the first time.

The stream had thawed almost completely when he got there. He sat down under a tree, the new leaves, barely opened, like a net of tiny florescent bulbs or fireflies in the four o'clock sky. Here a monk had found him the next morning, his back and head resting against the bleached trunk, the left leg stretched flat on the ground and the right hand hanging from the wrist on the raised knee. Such poise radiated from his form that the monk, as he sped up the hill, had thought better than to disturb the stranger. But returning an hour later, he had become suspicious. A deer grazed nearby unperturbed. The monk had rushed to the monastery and made the call.

Rosamund could barely control her nerves as she relayed the facts to me. In the end, she didn't wait for my response and disconnected abruptly. Outside, the line of cars had grown longer.

The crisis everywhere had worsened. A global depression that appeared almost coordinated: governments following each other's cues and acting in tandem. First squeeze, then ease up. This was all they ever knew, a kind of see-sawing they had perfected decades ago. But the trick had failed this time. Day by day one saw the old order come apart. Prices, already high, went haywire, and the industry continued to contract and slip into a death spiral.

Two weeks earlier, I had served notice on my flat and resigned my job. I wasn't willing to repeat what I had done back in my youth. Let someone else be strong and manage the despair and the layoffs. Two-thirds of my stock options were already worthless. But I had the family home in the hills to which I had made improvements over the years, and investments that hadn't completely gone to hell. There was money in the bank and silver in the vaults. With a little care, these could last a lifetime.

I stepped out on the terrace and smoked a cigarette in the rain. When one was over, I lit another. Pain had no purchase on me in that moment. I forced myself to not think of the past or the future. What had shattered inside could lie there undisturbed a while longer.

Before I could leave, I needed to make a clean break. To leave no loose ends and be gone for ever. That had always been the plan. What difference could it now make whether I saw Rita tomorrow or in a fortnight?

I flew direct to New York. The war in Europe made it unpredictable to travel via London or Frankfurt, to say nothing of Paris and Vienna.

A dark band hung low over the downtown skyline as it came into view across the Brooklyn Bridge. My thought immediately was of a building on fire. Passing beneath the gothic arches, I remembered my last trip nearly two decades ago. What a euphoric time that had been, filled with the wealth of big firms and the energy of youth! In those days, I worked for a subsidiary of the largest bank on Wall Street. After Lehman had gone down and the losses had stacked up, my bank wasn't the largest bank anymore. It was incredible to think that hardly two months before, one could have been forgiven for believing the music would never stop, that we would dance away our lives into oblivion.

The storm cloud passed; light got stronger. Bits of sky flashed between the buildings. But a mood of desolation remained in the wet streets. Several glass fronts along the sidewalks were boarded up. What had happened here? There was hardly a soul to be seen where once you had to jostle through the throng to get to the subway. Few cars came down Broadway. The bells of Trinity Church ricocheted two blocks and died quickly. I was glad to be moving uptown in the morning, to a small hotel on Madison Avenue near Central Park, away from this miserable atmosphere. Walking by the Bowery at dusk, I saw rats the size of rabbits scutter round the rustications of a deserted corner. Back in my room after an early dinner, I watched the glowing crown of the Woolworth—the slim mullions, the dramatic traceries and tourelles— accentuate the stark gloominess below. Most structures were pitch dark except near their tops where lights still burned in many windows as if all the town's denizens had gradually retreated to the upper stories, never to venture out again, conducting their affairs in isolation far above the septic streets. If things got any worse, I imagined them abandoning their expensive nests and escaping into the clouds.

I had called Rita earlier in the afternoon to let her know of my arrival. Now I dialed Rosamund, but she didn't answer.

Although she still worked in the City, some months before their daughter was born, Rita had persuaded Gir to move across the border into Connecticut. Now that she was not expected to be in office every day, there was less and less reason to live hemmed in by half empty buildings and the feeling of slow atrophy that had come to the place. And since being upstate in the valley for long stretches was not possible, she decided to build herself an idyll closer to Manhattan. The lease on their Midtown flat was flexible, so they shifted as soon as they had found a home of their liking. At the end of his teaching term, Gir would give up the place that had once brought them such joy and contentment. When classes were back in session, he would commute twice a week to deliver his lectures. But then the unexpected had happened, and the dream of family life, just at the edge of her fingertips, had gone up in smoke.

Her apartment was in a lovely complex nestled amid trees and parklands, and not far from Long Island Sound. It took me an hour from Grand Central to get there. I was in for a surprise. It wasn't Rita who opened the door for me but Gir's sister. I hadn't seen her in years. Her astonishment was as great as mine. Rita had told her nothing. So happy was she to see me that she forgot her grief. The very next instant she burst into tears on my shoulder. Rita walked into the room with little Lila in the crook of her arm. The child, all of four months, came to me easily. She had his eyes, big and liquid in that sweet face. The two women watched while I played with the girl. It was the first happiness I had known in months. There was great peace inside her aura. I didn't want the moment to end. Rosamund finally called and we spoke briefly before I passed the phone to Rita. I left with a promise to return in a couple of days.

I'd never had much to say to Rita. But now, in the face of tragedy, I found her poise and resilience impressive. She seemed completely in control of the situation. Only once did I detect a slight catch in her voice, when she told me how she had found Gir sobbing inconsolably late one night. Alarmed, she'd tried to comfort him. 'But he kept repeating in a low voice that he could bear no longer the loneliness of the red fox.'

Pockets of intense activity in an otherwise deserted East Side. Manhattan resembled a chessboard in the final throes of a game. Rosamund joined me a day later and we walked past block upon vacant block until we suddenly hit an intersection where there was the old energy of the city. Steam rose from the bowels of the earth at certain spots and people passed through it like in a Meyerowitz's photograph from the Seventies. The light too had the spectral quality of early film color, soft and granular, diffusing the flash of chrome into the shadows and making the streets recede in time. Someone had broken through the glass wall of the Flatiron Building and made a small fire inside. It was a terrifying sight. Hidden behind screens and scaffoldings, the abandoned structure poured out a musty darkness from its concavities.

'You sound just like him.' Rosamund said, collapsing on a bench at the northern end of Madison Square Park. She didn't say more, and I lit a cigarette. At night, she settled next to me in bed and talked until daybreak.

The sun's warmth lay in the pines as I approached the rambling house beyond the line of cedars that bordered the main road into the high mountains. The congested messiness of the town with its noise and tight despair lay safely at my back across the adjoining hill. I found the caretaker waiting outside the modern wing that I had help build while there were still members of my father's family living on the property. The man seemed not to have aged since my adolescence. I had always liked his air of seclusion and had requested him to stay on when the house had passed into my possession. Thin like a wraith, with graying short hair and skin that had turned pale with the years. But his gaze had retained the clarity of hermetic wisdom. He had prepared lunch and I ate in the dining area that looked south and was flooded with light at that hour. I had asked him to ready for me the room in the older part of the house, two stories up with windows opening in three directions and the oak floorboards dark with the patina of time. I fell asleep with the sun on my face and the sound of wind rushing through the conifers.

The light was dying when I woke up, but the faint brief outline of Nanda Devi was visible for the first time across the blue of distance, serenely floating above a ring of lower peaks to the north. I looked around and saw my childhood telescope on a tripod in one corner. I pulled the thing toward the window and thrust it halfway out into the open. Majestic and unsullied, the pink snow cone of the Bliss-Granting Goddess grew inside the eyepiece. There was hardly a breeze now, and in that deep silence, the sudden barking of a deer rose from the forested valley and startled me. It was followed by the trill of a passing cyclist, a bit of laughter. A man could live out his days in peace here and not lack or want for anything.

A scent of rain and lightning on young passionate bodies surprised by the elements on a tropical beach! I came awake thinking of Niki and found that it was indeed raining. A misty drizzle that carried the smell of wet earth, of woodsmoke and dripping undergrowth and rotting pinecones that Kipling had called the true smell of the Himalaya. But whose thought was this anyway? To Rosamund on that day in New York, I had sounded just like Gir. Now I felt my dead friend's energy permeate the room and his spirit slowly enter me, gently urging me to take on all his unlived days and years. I wasn't sure I was equal to the burden.

At noon, I went for a walk. For about five or six minutes I moved along the main road, then climbed some steps into the hillside and crossed a line of shops to where the stone alley gave way to a dirt track into the trees. Half a mile away was a breach in the forest where years ago I had spent a happy afternoon reading Gir's first, short book, proof already of his lonely intransigence in a crushingly banal world. The entire glowing range stretching east into Nepal could be seen from this point. Eagles rode the thermals into the clear sky, black specs against those dazzling slopes. I continued to stare at the mountains and the hours flew by as if they were minutes.

Later in the evening, waiting for dinner, I finally took the courage to retrieve from my backpack the two notebooks that Rita had handed me on our last meeting. *The Coach and The Spire*, Gir had written in his beautiful hand at the top of the first page. It was like calligraphy. I started to read but soon couldn't make out the words or their meaning, for my eyes had filled up with tears.

I closed the notebook and switched on the TV. The news was of yet another bank failure in America. Just three days prior, there had been a run on a big London bank. Before that a major investment bank had folded up in Zurich only hours after its chief executive had assured everybody that it had adequate reserves to cover its liabilities. This now was the fifth such bank to fail in two weeks. Where had one seen this film before? I turned down the volume and stepped out. A bird escaped through the net of cedar-silence cast upon a blue world. The image of the dark chevrons in the spire of the Chrysler Building flashed through my mind. Why had they not replaced the burnt-out lights in all the days I was there? A mere neglect on the part of the management? Or did it point to something larger? A kind of allegory for the slow atrophy of a nation's consciousness, its pride and its symbols.

Next day I tried reading the notebooks again. And again I could not go past a couple of paragraphs. The writing was clear, with few corrections or afterthoughts, but it held all the creative energy and deliberation of my friend's final years. The idea occurred to me that it might be easier, less emotionally taxing, if I were to read from a printed page instead. I told the caretaker I needed someone to do a little typing for me, that he should ask around when he was next in town.

It was a cruel sort of fate that brought the girl to the house. I wasn't ready yet for that kind of beauty: deep, delicate, utterly unassuming. She was exceedingly shy like people in the hills are known to be and barely looked at me when I addressed her. From the one-page resumé she handed me, I learnt that she was in her late twenties, although she looked even younger. I tried to engage her in conversation. With each passing minute, a strange kind of happiness began to take hold of me. Her skills included typing and stenography, and she had studied English and Accounting in college. If she spent but two hours a day on the manuscript, she would be done in less than a fortnight. I could urge her to go slow, to impress upon her the importance of the work, that she should check with me each time she had a doubt. But I was already starting to wonder what she could do once she was finished with the thing. In my eagerness, I promised a sum twice the going rate. Hearing this a look of slight confusion came over her, but she said nothing and nodded her acceptance of my offer.

We soon fell into a routine. She arrived at three and stayed till five. It was pleasant to watch her work, the sun in her hair, and on her long, fitted silk tunic, a different color each day. She would read a page or two with extreme concentration, a slight parting of the lips, and then type slowly into the computer. Behind her in the open window, the evergreens on the opposite hill sloped down thickly into the valley. Naturally, she avoided coming to me for anything.

On the fourth day, she appeared at the door while I was brewing tea. Once she had settled, I brought her a cup without first asking. It would have been too much to refuse, and to show her appreciation for my gesture, she struck up a conversation for the first time.

'New York,' she said, then paused briefly as if reconsidering. 'What kind of a place is New York?'

'A horrible miasma,' I replied without thinking. I don't know what had come over me. I was certain she would look up the word later and not approach me again. But she sensed I had slipped and allowed me to make amends. I asked about the town; told her I hadn't been there in years. She said people in town knew my family, that she herself had been in this house before. Was she bored with what she was doing? She shook her head, but I had the feeling she was holding back something. I left her to her work and went back to my reading.

After this, she warmed up to me, and we started to talk every day. Gir's steady, elegant writing gave way to strings of cool black letters that did not trouble the mind. I printed out the first part while she was completing the second and started to read. Snatches of conversation returned to me. Aspects of his life and experience I knew by heart were here touched by the magic of form and presented with a startling fullness that fitted the shape of the world. As always with him, the attention was on the pattern and not the material. The writing cleared the blind spots of memory, revealed connections till then hidden from view. In the space of a few hours, I watched fiction become truth and truth fiction.

Two weeks from the day I had met the girl, I got a call from Rosamund. The absurdity of the situation was crushing her. She said she couldn't stop wondering about Kalan, the old writer who had brought us close. That he must think Gir is still alive. 'We have to tell him, Herman,' she spoke the words slowly. 'You and I, we could go down the old ways, forget the world for a bit. Like we always talked of doing. I would give anything to see those mountains again. Will you come?'

I saw the long journey stretch before me. Winding down the hills into the burning plains I would go, then blaze away with her through the city traffic, crossing perhaps the very bar where we had first met sixteen years ago. I would hand her the typescript, and she would flip through the pages, read a line or two, and stare ahead at the road. The foothills would emerge again from the summer haze like patient and dusty giants. Soon we would be climbing into the mountains, ascending ridge upon ridge like ever taller waves upon a torrid sea. Along hairpin bends, now quick and steep and now slow and even, we would rise toward the sun as the last glimpse of flat earth fell away and vanished for ever. The high passes would spread beneath our wheels, and the ice crags, lined with minute waterfalls, would stand back a second to let us pass into that bare cold eternity at the knees of the gods.

I rolled her words in my head and thought of the girl who would be coming any minute now. Rosamund waited silently on the other end of the line. Then I heard the bells of the monasteries, felt the rush of the cold river through the sharp ravines, saw again the countless wildflowers softly swaying amid the rocky terrain.

'Yes,' I spoke into the phone. 'I will, yes.'

*　　*　　*

Aashish Kaul is the author of the chess-inspired novel *The Queen's Play*. He teaches at SUNY, Albany.